THE COUSINS

THE COUSINS

by

Jane Lester

Dales Large Print Books
Long Preston, North Yorkshire,
BD23 4ND, England.

British Library Cataloguing in Publication Data.

Lester, Jane
    The cousins.

    A catalogue record of this book is
    available from the British Library

    ISBN   978-1-84262-840-9 pbk

First published in Great Britain 1974 by
Robert Hale & Company

Copyright © Jane Lester 1974

Cover illustration by arrangement with Arcangel Images

The moral right of the author has been asserted

Published in Large Print 2011 by arrangement with
The Executor of Jane Lester, care of S Walker Literary Agency

Dales Large Print is an imprint of Library Magna Books Ltd.

Printed and bound in Great Britain by
T.J. (International) Ltd., Cornwall, PL28 8RW

Chapter One

The dazzling Spring sunshine caught the new yellow paint on Maria Ward, and made a fine background for the Sister's little pots of gold and purple crocus on the central tables, and the daffodils and tulips brought in by the patients last night.

They were mostly 'old hands' on Maria Ward, and Mrs Wooderson, in the first bed, got ready to help the quarterly intake of new young nurses from the PTS.

The two today were redheads. An appreciative and purely feminine gasp went up from the patients, most of whom had faded or grey hair. 'Twins!' Bed No.2 breathed.

The two girls beamed at her and denied it. 'No, cousins!' they laughed, and their laughter and good looks added to the splendour of the sunshine, the Spring flowers and the fresh clean paint and made life suddenly good.

'I'll put you right, ducks,' Mrs Wooderson breathed, as the Staff Nurse rustled in behind them. 'Ask me *anything!*'

But it was, in the end, a question of asking the two new ones a string of questions. They asked very little, and answered the women amiably enough. As always on a women's ward, the external things came first. Hair for instance. 'One of us is really red, the other dyed, and you have to guess which!'

The breath of life for women who had little hope of getting out of hospital this side of the summer holidays, at least.

'I'm Judy Blayne, and my cousin Linda Lawrence – we've been best friends since we left our prams. That's why they let us come on the same ward, because we work well as a team.'

'Well, you can say that again!' Mrs Wooderson said with a sigh. 'Best bed-make I've had for weeks. It's no fun when you weigh as much as I do, and you've got ham-fisted newcomers on the job,' and she smiled broadly, a very jolly smile.

'Why did you both decide to be nurses?' Miss Ramage asked. She was a teacher, and she could never persuade her girls to go into hospital to train.

'It's a long story.' The girls had reached her bed, and talked quietly, with half an eye for the Staff Nurse, who distrusted redheads. She had already told them so. 'We are both good at different things, and we wanted to work together, so we chose something we'd never thought of before – nursing.'

'But surely you must have both had a feeling for it,' Miss Ramage pressed, really wanting to know.

Linda said, 'One of us liked the domestic side, one of us was good at the theory. We pool our resources and get by.'

She had such a beautiful voice. Miss Ramage looked sharply at her. 'I shouldn't be surprised if you sing very well,' she remarked, and the girls laughed. 'And as to pooling your resources, you won't always be allowed to be together. What then?'

The new ones are the dogsbodies, Miss Ramage thought sadly, as she watched the girls all through that day, run off their legs. St Paul's was a big hospital, but it hadn't qualified for the new and expensive equipment that the new hospital at Skidgate was reputed to have. Those girls with the beautiful hands and the gay smiles would discover that there was no automatic bedpan cleanser and steriliser, and that washing was still done here by plunging the arms into suds. On her way to the bathroom, on her good days, she had seen the young ones, chatting cheerfully over their eternal mack scrubbing, rushing to the steriliser to rescue rubber gloves before they converged into a revolting splodge of twisted fingers, and that pretty little fair girl they had had, had been in tears over her efforts to clean the bathrooms. Work she had never had to do at home, she had confided. She had left.

Miss Ramage often wondered why the young nurses had to do such chores, and were expected to keep enough energy to learn all the medical names of diseases and instruments. When she had first come here, she used to hear one of the students say her instruments – the girl had spent her mid-week visiting hour with Miss Ramage, whose family was up north. The then Staff Nurse had stopped that.

The present Staff Nurse stopped other things, like the juniors being on full view in the wards when the doctors came round. Those beautiful redheads were hidden somewhere and kept busy. Miss Ramage thought, they'll find a chance to be seen. Those two won't be hidden for long!

The girls had a system. They took it in turns to do the things they weren't allowed to do together, so that one didn't get all the unpleasant things to do, or the disappointing times off. No authority yet had been able to fault that system. No authority yet had been entirely able to tell them apart, though together they didn't look identical. The girl with the beautiful voice could make hers deeper on occasion, to sound like the other one. They cultivated the same walk, the same way of tilting back the head. They weighed about the same, and off duty they dressed exactly alike. Since they had come to St Paul's the PTS had been a riot, and Sister Tutor had released them for general duties at the end of the three months with very mixed feelings: life would be more peaceful without them, but a little less interesting. One was quite exceptionally good at the practical things, the other was brilliant with the theory. The new bunch didn't begin to qualify for such work in either sphere.

The day after they started on Maria Ward, Richard Cartwright came back from his leave.

Judy saw him first, on her way to the X-ray department with a rush plate. She looked startled for a moment and then smiled broadly. Even twelve weeks in PTS hadn't taught the cousins to refrain from turning on their brilliant smiles at any man they saw without first ascertaining what his rank was. They had learned the ranks; they knew what a long white coat signified, and whether it had a breast pocket or not, and what a mere short white coat meant. They could even tell a dresser in Casualty from any other man. But it made no difference. If the cousins felt like smiling, they did, and their smiles could have a blinding quality.

Richard skidded to a halt. He was a tall young man with the kind of breath-taking good looks that made girls walk with their heads turned back to look. His colleagues could have said that his work didn't match his romantic and elegant appearance. He got out of any duty he could, and frankly said he had only become a doctor to please

11

his wealthy father, who was a manufacturing chemist who had dreamed in vain of becoming a medical man. Richard was very amiable, and a great favourite throughout the hospital, but he had a weakness for redheads.

'Well, we've got a little new one!' he said, leaning against the wall with his arms folded, and looking appreciatively at Judy's hair.

She put her finger to her lips in an enchanting warning gesture. 'Must rush with this wet plate. I'll be back in no time, if you want to wait,' and grinning at him she scuttled down the long alley-way and vanished round the corner. She had pretty legs, and a figure that even made the green checks of the First Years look trim and attractive. Richard waited.

But when she returned she was pushing a wheel chair and talking to the elderly patient. She appeared to have forgotten all about him.

He frowned, and then he decided to laugh at himself. This had never happened to him before. As she drew level, she said ruefully, 'Oh, sorry! Mrs Pepping was so cold. I thought I'd bring her back with me. See you sometime!' and she smiled broadly at him.

The patient chuckled. 'You're a one, duck! Don't you know who he is? Poor lad, that never happened to him before, I'll be bound!'

'Well, who is he?' Judy laughed.

Mrs Pepping was very happy to tell her. She had been six months on Maria Ward and in her heart she didn't believe she'd ever go home. She read a lot of love stories and kept her mind fixed on the romantic aspect of life so that she shouldn't remember the bleak future.

'He's just qualified and become a houseman on the medical side. He'll be that for six months, and they call him Dr Cartwright. His Christian name's Richard.'

'He looked rather young,' Judy murmured, laughing.

'He's not all that young,' Mrs Pepping chuckled. 'Twenty-four if he's a day and he's had three goes at passing his exams. No, he must be twenty-five at least. Well, I don't suppose he needs to work, since his Pa's so rich. They've got that great big house above the cliffs at Oakmere. Very nice place indeed, about two miles out of the town. And he's got a racing car and a yacht. But his Pa did so much want him to be a doctor.'

'Is he married?' Judy asked coolly.

'Oh, dear, no. He'll be a good catch for some lucky girl. Holidays abroad and everything she could wish for. What's your father, duck?'

'I haven't got any parents – neither has my cousin Linda. We lived with an old aunt until she died. She was a sweetie.'

'Well, take my advice and don't let Dr

Cartwright know you're both on your own, not till you know him better, that is,' she said. 'Oh, he's a nice enough young chap, but it's advice I give all the nurses, the pretty ones, that is. You'll see!'

Richard Cartwright came up to Maria Ward half an hour later. Sister said, 'Good gracious, Dr Cartwright, you here without me having to send a search party for you? Come along, Mrs Outram is—' and their voices tailed away as Richard swung down the ward, beside the fat little ward sister. Linda watched him from the door of the linen room. They had been split up for lunch. The ward sister didn't like redheads either, and decided she'd split them up for everything. It made her uneasy to have two nurses who looked so much alike.

Linda asked another junior who he was.

The junior didn't like him much. 'I know he's good-looking and rich and charming and all that, but he doesn't help, like some of the housemen do, and you get into trouble looking for him because if he doesn't feel like coming, he keeps out of the way. Give me a chap like Mr Addison, every time.'

'And who's Mr Addison,' Linda murmured, thinking about the way Richard Cartwright's eyes twinkled down at the little fat ward sister as she bullied him. Dr Cartwright was nice, she mused. If she'd gone in for that singing career she would have only had Professor James, who was bald and old and tetchy, even if he was clever. Linda passionately liked working with young men.

The other junior said firmly, 'Well, of course, Mr Addison isn't so young, because he's a senior surgeon and he's had to have time to get there, but he's a marvellous person.'

Linda decided it wasn't worth losing half of her lunch hour on the off-chance of seeing this Mr Addison go by, as the other junior intended to do.

It was Judy, after all, who saw Philip Addison, and that was through no fault of her own. She had been sent to another ward to pick up some files, and they all slithered out of her arms at Philip Addison's feet.

Normally he would have neatly side-stepped and pretended not to notice. He was a kind man, and the number of 'Green-checks' he had kept out of trouble through his tact was legion. But he couldn't take his eyes off Judy, so to prolong the moment he knelt and picked up her files. One was what he had been wanting, but had decided to go and get it himself. 'I'll take this,' he said, and smiled at her.

He had a rugged face. Judy thought of him as a kind elder brother and briefly wished she had one like this, but she smiled back at him and said she was sorry for being such an idiot.

'Scoot along with the rest, then, and I'll tell Sister I've taken this one,' he said.

It wasn't Judy's lucky day. She ran full tilt into Richard Cartwright as he came out of Sister's office, and dropped all the files again, but this time she had to pick them up herself. He was being *bleeped* and had to go. 'Sorry, my fault,' he murmured. 'I'll make it up to you later, and tell Sister it was my fault!'

The junior who had talked about him to Linda, saw that happen.

'That's as good an excuse as any for him to try to date you – I bet he said he'd make it up to you because Sister'll have it in for you now. She hates the files to be dropped and we're always dropping them, they're so slippery and the papers always fall out.'

Judy didn't answer. She was thoughtful. Never before had the cousins accepted a single date; they always went out with two men. But for the first time since they had come to the hospital, neither one of them wanted to do anything at the end of that long, long first day, other than lying full length on their beds with their feet up.

'Mutton stew and aching feet don't agree with me,' Linda said sleepily. 'And how can a girl go out after eating onions?'

'Did you want to go out?' Judy yawned. She had changed out of her uniform and

16

was pattering about in a shortie dressing-gown, her red hair tumbling to her shoulders.

'No. Never again in my life,' Linda moaned. 'I'd like to cut my feet off.'

It was a big room, shared by two other girls. Thelma Fraser was tall and dark and quiet, her serene pale face breaking into a small smile as she quietly flopped on to her bed and raised her feet. The fourth girl, Sheila Davey, lay flat on her chest. She had the comic face, a round dumpling face that had a rueful uptilt of eyebrows, the laugh always going against herself. Sheila was always in trouble, never did anything right, never got anyone but the odd man out, to make up the foursome with Thelma and her current boy-friend, who was the Casualty Officer. But Sheila's father was a GP and her mother had been a nurse, so ruefully she accepted her fate. She would have to be very bad indeed to be thrown out of the hospital. 'And I hate nursing,' she moaned.

'What do you want to do, then?' Linda asked, moving her eyes towards Sheila, without moving any other part of her, she ached all over.

'Me? Oh, I'd love to work on the land. Growing things. Open air. No need to rush for anything, that's me,' Sheila said, sadly.

Thelma looked anxiously across at her. 'Forget it, Sheil.'

Sheila shook her head. 'I could cry, honestly I could. Look at today – sunny, windy, good to be alive. Imagine the smells on the land. Earth on a Spring day. Damp leaves, in the woods. Try thinking of turning over soil that's *friable,* with a trowel, to put in a little rooted plant, heeling it in. Oh, gosh, I wish I was dead – all I can smell at this moment is ether and disinfectant and soap – the kind in the sluice. Honestly, most of my life is spent in the sluice. I have to do everything over twice. And bless me, when I go home, the surgery's got practically the same smells, except old papers and dust and the polish on the mahogany furniture that was there when my grandfather was our town's GP.'

'How awful!' Linda said feelingly, and her eyes met Judy's. Is that how they would get in the end? They'd forgotten smells, when they were in the PTS. Life had just been a continuation of school, and good fun. Lectures, but then both of them loved the lectures. And there'd been the visits to places – that model farm which looked more like a factory than anything else, and even the sewage place hadn't been all that bad, because the statistics had caught the imagination of the cousins.

'Don't!' Thelma said again, sharply, this time. 'Don't put these two off, anyway. They're good at it! Besides, it's only because you've got the blues today. Tell you what –

let's have a party.'

Sheila brightened. 'Oh, yes, what a good idea. What will it be for, though?'

'To celebrate the appearance of these two,' Thelma said firmly. 'I'll rustle around for some guests, and they've each got to bring something towards it. Shan't be long.'

She went out at once. Sheila slid off the bed and ran a comb through her hair. 'Gosh, I'm hungry at the mere thought of it!'

'How can we have a party?' Judy asked slowly. 'I thought we were supposed to be quiet and orderly in our rooms?'

'Well, you see, there's a system. We post someone on the door, and she says when Home Sister is in sight. Being at the end of the corridor, you can get good warning. And then everyone gets out the notebook they've brought, and shoves the grub and drink under their chair. You're allowed to study in big bunches, on this floor, so we can manage like that! We've had six parties already.'

In the end Home Sister didn't come, and they weren't too noisy. They drank cocoa and ginger pop and fizzy lemonade without much anguish afterwards; someone brought in a cake she had had from home that day, and the rest had an accumulated assortment of tinned food and bars of chocolate. Judy was sure they'd all be sick but Linda had no such qualms; she never did. Watching her cousin, Judy thought for the first time how little everything seemed to affect her. She wondered if Linda had caught sight of Dr Cartwright, and if her cousin's heart had turned over and hammered painfully against her ribs as her own had.

Judy didn't think so. Perhaps Linda hadn't even seen him. She herself had been rather alarmed at the sensation that young man produced, especially on the second occasion. It said nothing that she had managed to look cool and casual; she could look anything she liked, but she had a turbulent set of emotions inside that eternally bothered her. Most of all was the overwhelming generosity she often felt, whether of emotions or in the practical way of a service or personal possessions. Linda wasn't like that. The only comfort Judy got from this was the sure knowledge that Linda would never be hurt, as she herself had been, often, and was likely to be.

During the party, a girl called Katie Sutcliffe, who was apparently the one who had the mischievous ideas on this floor, said, 'Dear Dr Cartwright is back, and has seen a redhead that's new.'

'Oh, which one?' everyone clamoured. Richard Cartwright was choosy, as by right; he was every girl's darling.

'I don't know,' Katie said, laughing and watching first one cousin and then the other, for give-away reaction. When neither of the cousins appeared concerned, Katie said, 'I told him they were identical twins, just for the fun of it, but he wouldn't believe me. He said, "Two of them? What rot! Of course there aren't – I would have heard about it before!" so what do you think everybody – I vote that we keep it dark that there *are* two of them!'

Everyone thought it a good idea. This set were the rebels against Authority, and tore it down when possible. To tease a doctor was the height of good fun, especially as it was someone like Richard Cartwright. 'But how can we?' Thelma objected. 'They always go about in pairs, don't you?'

'Not always, apparently,' Katie said. 'Which one of you was it he talked to – twice, apparently. Or was it one each time?'

Linda looked at Judy, but Judy said shortly, 'I wish you wouldn't. We have fooled about in the past, but not here. This is too serious – isn't it?' she appealed to her cousin.

Linda half closed her eyes. 'Oh, I don't know. On further consideration I think it might be fun. That way, we can both have him. We've never hunted alone, always in pairs, and that's the only way to continue … don't you think?'

Judy looked surprised, and shrugged, saying it didn't matter. Katie Sutcliffe thought,

21

'Oh, this is fun. So it was Judy he saw both times, and Linda didn't even know about it and is going to play rough!'

'Well, that's the order of the day, girls. Let's keep them apart all the time, and play it strong that there's only one of them. Dear Richard's had it coming to him for a long time.'

'Why do you say that?' Judy asked.

Katie shrugged. 'A couple of nurses, at least, have taken him seriously in this last year, and been badly hurt in the process. Personally I'd like to see him have a taste of his own medicine, and as far as I can see, this is a heaven-sent way to do it.'

After the party was over, and lights were out, the steady deep breathing of Sheila and Thelma prompted Linda to say softly into the darkness, 'You asleep, Judy?'

Judy wasn't. She knew that. In many ways, the cousins had developed that unbelievable closeness that only twins have. Judy said, 'No, not yet. Why aren't you?'

'Thinking. We've never split up yet.'

'No, I know. I don't like it either.'

'Then you're not ... special ... about this Richard person?'

'I've only seen him twice, and each time I was at a disadvantage – especially the last time when I upset the files,' Judy said shortly, and prayed that Linda, who knew her so well, wouldn't guess how the excitement rocked her even at the thought of him bending over her and finally going off to see who was 'bleeping' him, and leaving Judy to pick up all the papers.

Linda said, 'You sound as if you mean anything but that!' Judy sighed. Sometimes it was uncomfortable, belonging to someone who knew you so well. 'Well, I can't help that. I have seen him – I agree he's terribly handsome and charming but at the moment all I want is to go to sleep. I'm nearly dead.'

'No, don't let's sleep. Let's discuss this. They talk about him. He must be quite something. I don't want to go out with him in a foursome. I vote we each take him in turns, share him.'

Judy thought, with a little frightened flutter, how could you share a man with someone else, when that man could make you such a shivering jelly of consternation and anticipation? 'I couldn't, not with any man, not share him, I mean,' Judy said firmly. 'We never did that before: why try to do it now?'

'It's an experiment,' Linda said firmly, and when she said that, there wasn't any real peace until it happened, because it left her the option of making the other person seem unreasonable. 'All right,' Judy sighed and turned over and went to sleep.

Thelma wasn't asleep. She listened unashamedly because in a sense she was the responsible one, the leader of this room and she didn't want trouble. And she could foresee nothing but trouble if those two did what Linda had just so firmly suggested. Linda, Thelma thought dispassionately, was not going to be the sort of girl she herself could like an awful lot, which was a pity. So uncomfortable when sharing a room in the Nurses' Home.

Chapter Two

Most of the women on Maria Ward came to that conclusion, too, in a very short time. Linda was the brains of the pair, Judy the one with the comfortable manner, the kind hands, the one who thought of one's comfort with the same intuitive sense, as if it were for her own comfort. The women liked to have Judy do things for them, and most of them learned to tell the two girls apart. They also discovered that Linda had a curious, slightly malicious streak in her that made her be there, when they wanted Judy.

But the girls remained happy and entertaining, a delight to have on the ward. The women missed them on their times off.

Richard Cartwright, curiously, didn't discover that there were two of them at first. His habit of keeping out of the way when there was work to be done, was partly responsible for this. Maria Ward was the least exciting of wards for a doctor. The things that went wrong were predictable, and they wore the same old faces. Richard yearned for his Casualty stint. There was real interest in that department.

The first time he dated Judy was the day

his new sail craft was to be taken out to The Point. 'Are you a good sailor?' he wanted to know.

'Fair,' she admitted.

'Crew me?'

'If you like,' she said cautiously. 'How big is she?'

'Oh, it's not the 45-footer,' he assured her. 'The Sea Queen needs at least four to crew her. No, the Baby Dolphin is just right for two people on the spree,' and he showed her the map.

Oakmere was five miles from the hospital. The way to the Basin was ten miles more, where his craft was moored. 'She's a honey,' he said, smiling, and he managed to make it sound as if that description also applied to Judy.

This was the crunch, she thought. Linda said carefully, as she sat polishing her nails, 'So you're going sailing with him. That's as well, as I'm a rotten sailor. Make sure you're not too enthusiastic, though, and don't be too efficient, in case I get landed with a sea trip on a calm day. I shall want a get-out for not doing the right things.'

'Study that book I gave you, then,' Judy said carelessly, but she was worried. She was raging inside against Linda's cool assumption that she would be willing to share Richard with her, and Judy had never felt like that towards her cousin in her life.

Linda looked critically at Judy's neat navy slacks and the trim sweater. 'I say, do put on something a little more trendy,' she begged, so Judy let her fix a scarf that was more Linda's taste than her own. She could take if off before she met Richard, she thought. Linda said, as a parting shot, 'Don't forget, me next time, and bags I that smart roadster of his – that's what I want to do – try that beauty out, with him.'

Judy nodded and went out. Of course, they should both break it off before it got any further. What would happen if and when he discovered there were two of them? If he didn't feel too badly about the trick played on him, which one would he choose and what would it be like between them after that? Could she bear to give him up to Linda, Judy asked herself? She had known him such a little while, yet she knew the answer would be no. It scared her.

On the way out of the Nurses' Home, she tore off the orangy scarf, and stuffed it in her pocket, getting out a navy one with white polka dots on, and tying it round her hair. The wind blew it across her eyes, so she didn't at first see Philip Addison get out of his car. In black jacket and striped trousers, he looked different anyway; less approachable.

She stared up at him, trying to place him, the sun still in her eyes. His voice told her who he was.

'Where are you off to?' he said.

'Sailing, sir, with Dr Cartwright.'

His sensitive mouth turned down a little at that. '*Are* you a sailor?' he asked, and when she admitted that she was, he pursued, 'How's your swimming?' so she said it was fair, to Life Saving Standards. Only then did he seem satisfied.

'Well, take care. The currents beyond Oakmere aren't funny, and I believe you're a stranger to the district.'

'I'll be all right, sir,' Judy said, and slipped past him. Funny, as soon as she got away from him she couldn't remember what he looked like: Richard's face blotted him out.

Richard was waiting and impatient. 'Take that scarf off and let the wind rip through your hair,' he ordered, but she smilingly refused. It wasn't her strong point to look wind-blown; that was Linda's special thing. Linda's hair had a tight curl in it, that made it behave in the worst weather. Judy knew her limitations.

Richard tried to take it off while he was driving. She said, with no great pleasure in her voice, 'I like a careful driver,' so somewhat surprised, he raised his eyebrows, tried to be cross and couldn't, and finally laughed and said he'd be good.

'Funny thing, sweetie,' he said, 'that isn't the first time I've had a mind to be cross with you and I found I couldn't. What are you – a witch?'

She just smiled at him.

'Don't you want to know when the other occasion was?'

She shook her head. 'But I expect you'll tell me!'

'Well I'm dashed! Look here, I've thrown girls over for less than that!' he said indignantly. 'You remember that!'

'Dr Cartwright,' she said, still smiling, 'I'm not all that bothered!' and while he looked more surprised and put out than ever, she asked herself in bewilderment how she could talk so coolly when her heart was thumping madly at the mere thought of his throwing her over, perhaps for the more sophisticated treatment which he would surely get from Linda.

She was so obsessed with this thought, that she forgot Linda and her injunction not to show too much skill when it came to being crew on his little craft.

It was just the size that appealed to Judy, and it was a very plushy craft. Everything that money could put into a small model, had been put, and she had been built for speed as well as beauty.

'You like her, don't you?' Richard said, in a pleased way.

She nodded, and smiled, and kept her attention on what she was doing.

'You don't waste words, do you?' he said. 'Here, take this sheet – catch!'

Luffing across the mouth of the Basin, they were both absorbed but once out in the open sea, breasting the really choppy surface of the water, he saw she wasn't going to be seasick and again approved. Too many promising affairs with pretty nurses had finished in disgust after a sharp wind across the Point.

'Who taught you to handle sail?' he asked her.

'Does it matter? I love it, if that's what you want to know, Dr Cartwright.'

'Oh, I say, do chuck it and call me Rick. All my friends do.'

She nodded, and let the point go.

'What made you become a nurse?' he asked her.

'I wanted to,' she said briefly.

'And you're good at it. I hear it from even our dear Sister on Maria Ward, and that is no mean praise. She was watching you the other day and said most grudgingly, "That girl is good".'

Judy looked startled. Had it been herself or Linda? 'What are you looking like that for?' he asked, watching the look. 'You *are* an odd girl. Every other girl I know would have simpered and said, something like, "No, really, Rick, did she? What else did she say, Rick?" But not you! You just look at me as if I'm a prize fathead to bother to report the incident at all.'

'I didn't mean to, if it's true I did,' Judy laughed.

'What do your parents think of your progress? or don't you tell them?' he demanded. He wanted to get some idea of her background, but it was just as if a white sheet had been hung up behind her, and there was nothing, nothing at all to tell him where she had come from or what her home life had been like.

'Oh, let's not talk of things like that,' Judy begged. 'Let's discuss sail – how many small craft have you owned?'

It was, though she hadn't intended it for anything but an escape, a smart move. He was always interested in talking about that particular subject. As a sailing enthusiast, Judy made a new assessment of him. He was spoiled by his family's wealth to the extent that he didn't bother to work unless he was forced to, but where sailing was concerned he worked, very hard. He gave everything he had to it, and perhaps Philip Addison's warning about Richard was not justified, but merely based on what he knew of the young man in the world of hospital. Judy and Richard talked happily about boats and messing about in them, until he decided it was time to eat. He chose the island.

'Magnus Island? But isn't that private

property?' Judy objected, frowning.

'It is, but it happens to belong to people we know. So it's all right. Oh, don't look like that, Judy – if you must know, my guvnor is doing his level best to buy the place.'

She silently crewed for him while he gave orders, and they ran into the tiny natural harbour. It was a beautiful spot. She looked round at it in sheer delight, but his wealth and his constant careless references to it bothered her.

He had a good stock of food on board. He built a little fire of dry twigs and erected a tripod of branches of it and showed her how to make kebabs from things out of tins and to cook sausages in tin foil among the hot ashes.

'Where have you been all your life, if you've never done this before?' he wanted to know.

She shook her head. She never had been able to talk about her childhood. 'Just take it that I've had no fun – at least, not this free and easy sort of fun – and I'm very willing to learn how. Do you think I'll make a good pupil?'

'An excellent pupil!' he said readily, then laughed. 'You're blushing – you really are!'

She couldn't stop her face from getting hot. That, too, was a thing that had always happened to her, never to Linda. And with hair that colour, it wasn't pretty. She was cross. 'It's the way you look at me,' Judy said, looking away.

'Perhaps I'm looking at you for a reason,' he said.

'You're a great tease, Richard, and I wish you wouldn't be.'

'Then I won't tease. I'll be in deadly earnest and do something I've wanted to do since the first moment I set eyes on you.'

'What's that?' she asked unwisely.

He leaned forward and kissed her. It wasn't a savage kiss, but it was too loaded with everything she didn't like, to be called a gentle one. She pulled away, frowning. 'Don't. Don't do that!' she said sharply.

'Don't do that ... what? Don't do it because I'm me and you would rather it were someone else? Or don't do that because you're playing hard to get, and would like me to think you don't like kissing?'

'Just ... don't do that,' she said. She lifted pained eyes to his. They were velvety, very dark brown, and very steady. He was puzzled because they had no malice or fun or studied innocence – they were just steady and serious and made him feel he'd done something not quite right, which he didn't like at all.

'Oh, have a heart, Judy! You surely don't expect to go out with a fellow and not get kissed – with looks like yours?'

'I can't explain. It's just that I feel that I

personally want to save kissing for the special man in my life. I have nothing against kissing, nor against other girls if they like to kiss all over the place. It's just that I don't like it, personally.'

'Why, you stuffy little urchin!' he exploded, and taking her into his arms, he kissed her thoroughly and long. She gave up struggling and did the next best thing, pretending to be a marble statue. It was effective. He put her away from him at once and looked extremely annoyed. 'You *are* playing hard to get, aren't you?'

'If that's what you think,' she said in a pained way, getting to her feet, 'then I'd like to go back. It's no use. The whole picnic is spoilt.'

'Yes, it dashed well is, because you can't walk back to the mainland and that means I shall have to pack up all this stuff and take you.'

'I can swim,' she said shortly, and walked towards the shore.

After a minute, he got up and raced after her. 'Oh, Judy, for goodness' sake, don't let's. We're not children! All right, I'll play it your way, but I bet if I stop being amorous, you'll want it. Girls are like that!'

She looked calculatingly at him.

'*Now* what's going on in that head of yours?' he demanded.

'I'm a little scared,' she confessed. 'I'm not

usually wrong about people, but I seem to have been about you.'

'What did you think I was like, for heaven's sake? Anyway, you've only got to ask anybody at the hospital. I believe I am Playboy No.1.'

'I know. That's why I preferred to make up my own mind about you' she said, and she sounded hurt in an odd way. 'I was wrong.'

'Did it matter?' he asked quietly. 'Does it matter now?'

She wanted so badly to be able to shrug and say it didn't matter but she couldn't. 'Yes,' she said briefly.

'Now you've put me on the wrong foot and no chap likes that!'

'I can't help that, Richard. What did you think I was like?'

'Easy, like any other girl. Why not? All girls are easy. You really would be surprised at the lengths the nurses will go, to get in the queue for a date with old Richard, and it's sickening at times.' He shrugged. 'But they're all good for a petting party.'

'What a wasted date for you, Richard. Come on, I will at least help you pack up the things.'

Perversely he wouldn't let her. 'No, let's eat. That's the trouble. We're hungry. Let's eat, and talk. I want to know a bit more about a girl who isn't dying for me to kiss her. It's a sad sock in the jaw for me, I can tell you! I really must be slipping.'

He was right about their hunger though. Sitting one each side of the fire, they ate heartily of the things he'd cooked. 'At home there's an old poacher who showed me how to do all this,' he confided. 'When I was a boy he used to take me out with him and show me how to snare a rabbit and roast it, and it tasted good, ever so slightly smoky, but good! Sometimes he'd do a stewpot like the gypsies do, putting a bit of everything in it. He had a pal who was a tramp, and there they'd sit, with me on the other side, a miserable shrimp of a junior I was in those days, listening wide eyed to the tales they told. But if you ever want a stew that's heavenly, there's nothing like one made of chicken and rabbit and bird – any kind of bird – with any root vegetables you can find, and a handful of herbs.'

But Judy wouldn't exchange confidences. No matter how much he told her about his own life.

'Oh, come on, I've told you about my home up there on the cliff and the family – I want you to meet my sister – you'd like her! Just the two of us, and our parents and grandfather, and a staff that's kept running a house that's too big for us. Now why won't you swap a few confidences? Was your home a cottage or a flat in town – surely you can tell me that?'

She unbent a little, but not nearly enough for his liking. All she would say was, 'It was a house, a tall narrow Victorian house, and everything in it smelt of dust.' That was to make herself believe that she was forgetting it. But she wasn't. She missed it more and more, and she missed their aunt, who had appeared vague and eccentric, but who could prove herself very shrewd on occasion and very good for sorting out the problems of the young. And although everyone said she liked Judy more than she liked Linda, the aunt never allowed it to show. Now it was all gone and they were on their own, she and Linda, and it grieved her more and more every day to find that Linda not only didn't care, but probably never had cared. Linda could turn on the charm for anyone, and she had turned it on for her aunt. But she hadn't loved her. Judy had loved her because she stood in place of their parents. Judy had to have someone to love. Linda was all she had at the present moment, and Linda had a curious cool curtain around her that repelled all other people's affection.

'Now what are you dreaming about?' Richard demanded.

'Trying to turn back the clock,' she smiled. 'Stupid thing to do!'

'It *is* a stupid thing to do,' he agreed. 'Does it hurt so much – remembering whatever it is you were remembering?'

It was the first time he had sounded tender, thinking about somebody else. A knife turned in her heart. Was this being in love? Loving someone in spite of knowing that he was free and easy with all girls, on his own admission? She hoped not.

'Yes, it hurts. I don't want to look back at all. Do you think we could swim? I think I'd like that.'

'All right.' They stood up, and he put his hands on her shoulders. 'No, don't flinch away. I'm not going to kiss you. I want to ask you something. Answer me a question: are you a twin?'

'No!' she said in surprise, forgetting that the others had said it would be a good joke to kid him along.

'Have you got a sister?' he insisted

'No!' she said, and couldn't make up her mind whether to tell him about her cousin or not. But it had been her instinctive habit all her life, not to give confidences if she could help it. What was the good of a private hoard of personal memories if you were going to tell anyone else about them? And until she was more sure of Richard, she didn't want to share any of those memories with him. So the moment passed, and the opportunity lost.

'One more question: are you really telling me the truth, about not liking being kissed? Or are you just putting me on, so you can go and tell all your friends that you kidded me along and I didn't get any kisses and I must be slipping?'

'Oh, for goodness sake!' she burst out in pure irritation. 'Of course it's the truth! Do you set such a store on your reputation as every little nurse's No. 1 Pin-up Boy that you have to make sure you reduce every girl to a shivering jelly dying to be kissed by you? Is that it?'

He was silent for a moment. 'Good enough,' he said at last. 'I believe you really mean it. I'd like to be sure you won't tell the others, though. You don't know what a hell girls can make for a chap like me, though, in hospital. Once you get a reputation for being a romantic kind of chap, you've had it. You have to keep it up, even though it bores you stiff.'

'Don't tell me kissing bores you!' Judy said scathingly.

He had the grace to grin. 'Not most times, though sometimes it does, when a girl doesn't turn out to be as interesting as she promised at first.'

Judy turned away, biting her lip on a retort. Richard said, 'I believe you would like to say I make you sick!' and he sounded so amiable about it that she had to laugh.

'Well, yes, you do.'

'What did you expect of today then?' He was genuinely blank.

She turned round on him. 'Sailing, of course. I love it. Swimming, I love that too. And both are things one likes to indulge in with a congenial companion.'

'But that's not all,' he said shrewdly.

Briefly her eyes looked not far from tears. 'No, you're right, it's not all, and I could kick myself for it, though it won't help. I never did believe in the theory of falling in love without being able to help one's self, but it seems that it is just a chemical reaction after all, and I can assure you, I'm loathing myself for having been just another victim.'

Chapter Three

Kneeling on the ward floor the next morning, with the rest of the nurses, for morning prayers, Judy asked herself what she should do. As she had admitted to Richard, she loved him, not from choice, not in competition with the others, but because she couldn't help herself. That confession had bothered him so much that he hadn't attempted to kiss her any more. Nor to make a further date with her. But the ache was still there inside her, and if she did nothing further, and she heard that he was dating other girls, what would life here be like?

The nurses knelt with their hands behind their backs. The times might change, fashions come and go, young people opt out of going to church, but all the time the Sister of this ward was Sister Curzon, ward prayers would be the same. Serious, sternly supervised, a little longer than the prayers on any other ward, and in an odd way, the most comforting prayer gathering that Judy had ever known.

She would have liked to look at Linda to see how she was taking it, but then, she told herself helplessly, who could tell what Linda

41

was thinking about anything, least of all herself?

After prayers, the giant wheel of the hospital day comfortingly continued where prayers left off. Judy could have wished that she hadn't fallen in love so soon on her entering the hospital, because it would have been good to work here, good to be able to count the years ahead, as long as her health and strength lasted, to feel that here was security, the sense of being surrounded by other people who didn't just live and breathe, but who were engaged in a grim battle against ill health, injury and death.

Linda had looked speculatively at her on her return yesterday but had said nothing. Neither had the others. But today it was different. Somehow the patients had got to hear of it.

'Went out with that Dr Cartwright, didn't you, duck; yesterday? Did you like it then?' Mrs Wooderson wheezed, as the girls made her bed.

Linda flicked a glance up at her cousin as if waiting for the answer. Judy said, casually, 'Yes, because it was sailing. I adore sailing.'

'Cor, you never like that, do you, duck? But you might get washed overboard and drown-ded!'

That made both the girls laugh. 'Not our Judy,' Linda said. 'She's the water-baby –

she's like a fish in the water. You should see her!'

'And you're not? How's that, then?'

Linda laughed. 'Well, some people like the water, others just tolerate it. There you are!'

'Well, I must say I've never done more than paddle in me life, and I don't know as I'd care to be right in it!' Mrs Wooderson said, and then did her usual big sigh of content as Judy finished her off. Linda had already turned to the next bed. A patient couldn't hold Linda's interest for very long.

Miss Ramage had been worrying about them again. 'They say you two are going to play up that Dr Cartwright,' she said. 'I do wish you wouldn't. He's been around. And he's such a favourite that he doesn't care. One nurse is much the same as another to him!' she finished earnestly, but it was at Judy that she was looking.

'Don't worry about us,' Linda said lightly. She meant, don't make a pet of Judy or you'll hear from me!

Miss Ramage said, 'I think someone should worry about you!' but again it was Judy she looked at.

That day when they went off duty, they were roped in to join the Social Club. Linda was very keen on tennis and badminton and Judy good-naturedly played along. But this was for the entertainments side. 'We do a quarterly concert for the patients and staff.

Now, what can you two do?' the Casualty Officer asked.

Thelma said, because she was afraid they would both deny being able to do anything, 'Linda sings and Judy can play the piano – I've heard her.'

'I only tried the big grand,' Judy protested, but it was no use. So she let Bobby Jeeves put her name down, and Linda said, after a moment's hesitation, 'Well, if I must, I must, but I am not going to let it stop me going out if I want to!' She smiled as she said it and Bobby thought she was just appearing not to want to push herself forward, but Thelma thought, I bet you would never let it interfere with anything you wanted to do.

Bobby Jeeves had a wide good-natured grin. He was tall and skinny as a rake but he had never been known to scowl or show bad temper and his disposition was perfect for Casualty. Perfect for running the Social Club, too. He put every ounce of energy into whatever he was doing, and Judy, at least, wasn't surprised when he roped them in for rehearsals that day when they came off duty.

Linda said nothing. Judy worriedly said, 'It's all right for you, isn't it, Lin?' and her cousin smiled and said, 'We still hunt in pairs, I believe? Nothing's changed, has it?' which meant that she was including Dr

Cartwright, and that the next date would be hers.

The room in which the grand piano was, had long windows all down one side. One thing this hospital had, Judy saw with pleasure, was a concern for the off duty of its staff. The social angle was very good. She sat down at the grand and it was very good, in tune and a delight to play.

On this particular day they had the whole afternoon off and Bobby Jeeves ran through the programme, keen to get started. He had roped in all the people who could play an instrument, and a curious hotchpotch they were, Judy thought, with amusement. One of the students had a huge harmonica and there were two concertinas. Sheila Davey muttered, 'Oh help, look what my treasure's bringing in' and there was a general laugh. The big clumsy lad that had already been pointed out to Judy as Sheila's make-weight – the one she got landed with every time there was a foursome – had a home-made one-man band which took five of them to bring in. He sat down at it and made nice and funny noises that set the tone of the afternoon.

'Where's your Linda?' Sheila asked, but Linda couldn't be found. Judy said uncomfortably, 'She'll be along. She went back for her handkerchief or something.'

Thelma looked sharply at Judy. 'Who were

you on the telephone to? Don't mind me asking, but we're not supposed to take private calls in the Nurse's Home.'

'It was Dr Cartwright,' Judy said quietly. 'He wanted me to meet him but I said we were rehearsing.'

Sheila heard that. 'You turned him down, for this?'

Judy said steadily, 'I explained that I'd already promised. There are other times when we can go out.'

Sheila burst into explosive laughter and looked as if she were going to tell everyone. Judy caught her arm. 'Don't mention it to the others. Don't make a joke of it, please!'

'Why not? It'd go all over the hospital and that lad needs to be taken down a peg or two! Oh, do let me tell the rest of the girls – they'll love it!'

'Please, no,' Judy said earnestly. 'I'll never tell you anything again if you insist. It means a lot to me.'

'Oh, I didn't know you were all that keen on him, so soon. Why didn't you say?' Sheila retorted, going red.

'No, I didn't mean that,' Judy said painfully, trying to find the right words. 'I meant that it means a lot to me not to betray anyone, even Richard. I was cross with him but I wouldn't say or do anything to make people laugh at him. That kind of cruel joke doesn't appeal to me. Hope it doesn't sound stuffy.'

Sheila stared at her. 'I say, you're not half bad, are you?' she said at last. 'Okay, I get the message. Don't clobber anyone behind his back just for the fun of it. I agree! I suppose we all do it but it's decent of you to think of it. That's our trouble – we just don't think! But I tell you what – I bet your Linda hasn't got those kind of scruples.'

'I don't like back-swipes at Linda, either,' Judy said quietly. 'Not even from my friends,' which softened it a little.

Bobby's personality bred enthusiasm, and Judy's playing was of a higher standard than anyone had expected. 'Why didn't you opt for a musical career, then?' Thelma asked her.

'Because we wanted to be together,' Judy said simply, and for her, that was the truth. Thelma wondered what Linda had had in mind, coming to study nursing. They had yet to hear the golden voice which Judy insisted that Linda had.

The rehearsal room was near the Men's Wing. Half way through, one of the Sisters poked her head round the door. 'Who was playing the Rubenstein bit?' she asked, raking them with an experienced eye which finally alighted on Judy, although she was sitting on the floor by the radiogram sorting through records at the time.

Bobby strolled over to her and told her.

'Well, I've got a request to make. We've a

patient who's prognosis is short but he heard the Rubenstein and wants it played again. I just wondered if we could arrange it by opening widows, though it's cold in the ward. Oh, you know the chappie, Mr Jeeves – it's the spinal case you brought up from Cas. last Friday from Jennetts Cross.'

'Well, I don't know, Sister – what about that old upright piano that's still on that floor? A couple of us could wheel it in, if it wouldn't upset the other chaps.'

She was delighted. 'They'd love it. I suppose Nurse Blayne would oblige?' and Bobby said, grinning, 'Oh, that's no problem.'

The upright piano had been left in an alcove after the Christmas festivities. There was a two-wheeled trolley they used to slip under it and push it around. It had been all over the hospital for their carol singing. A battered case but still surprisingly good, Judy found, as she sat down to it.

Her hair was a target for all the men's eyes, and then she began to play, and there wasn't a sound. Even old Granfer Smith stopped rustling his bag of apples.

After she had played an encore, the ward sister shook her head at Judy, to play no more. So she asked if she could speak to the patient.

He looked pitifully young, she thought, to be knowing he was to die so soon. She said, 'I'm afraid I'm a bit rusty, but now I know I can get at a piano, I'm going to put some time in on it.'

'It was ... beautiful,' he said painfully. 'Some more? Maybe ... tomorrow?'

'I'll ask Sister, shall I?' she beamed at him.

After that, she had to go round the ward to say a word or two to the other men, collecting a nod of permission from the ward sister first.

The Staff Nurse murmured to the Sister, 'There are two of them, one of them is being dated by dear Richard.'

'Which one?' the ward sister asked sharply. She knew only too well what Dr Cartwright was like.

'Difficult to tell if you don't know them, Sister, but the grapevine has it that it's that one!'

'Oh, no,' Sister Nairn murmured.

While Judy was on that ward, the other nurses went to find Linda. Sheila reported, 'She's not anywhere! Anyone got any ideas as to where she is?'

'Plenty,' Kate Sutcliffe said. 'That new porter on the gate saw her go out with dear Richard!'

'Oh, so he knows there are two of them,' Sheila was disappointed. She had wanted a good joke at his expense.

'Not necessarily,' Katie said, laughing quietly. 'It seems dear Linda went out in Judy's scarf – you know they dress alike except for the odd etcetera – and she had sun glasses too, and if I hadn't known where Judy was, from where I was standing the other day it looked just like Judy, the way she walked, so maybe she's doing her Judy act today and having a good joke at his expense. The thing is – who do we dislike most – dear Richard or dear Linda? A show of hands, please!'

'No, here comes Judy,' Thelma warned. 'Now I know how you all feel, but don't let Judy know.' She frowned. 'Richard will know!'

Richard might be smart enough to see through Linda's light disguise, she prayed, because that young man would be unforgiving if he were made to feel a fool, and he would believe only too readily that Judy had been in the plot too.

Richard had been very put out when Judy had refused to come out with him that day. 'I thought you wanted to go for a spin in my new car?' he asked in an aggrieved voice.

'Well, I did,' Judy had said regretfully, 'but I have already promised the Casualty officer I'd rehearse with them and I've always found it a good rule to stick to the first engagement, not break it for something I might like better.'

'Break it!' he had ordered, and was quite surprised when Judy didn't fall in with his imperious command. Other girls had liked to be ordered to break a date to be with him.

He was sure she would alter her mind, so he hung about and when he saw Linda strolling towards him, head flung back just like Judy's, and sun glasses on, he grinned softly to himself. So he was right! She was just like the others.

'So you did come! Good girl!' he approved, putting out a hand to her.

Linda let him take her hand. She had a warm feminine hand with beautifully manicured finger-tips, and small wrists that she liked to adorn with bracelets. Never rings on her fingers, never a wrist watch, but bracelets. She collected them, mainly presents from the men in her life. She liked good things and she had an unerring instinct for what was right to wear, yet wearing just a little more than any other girl would. The bracelets struck a chord in Richard's mind, but although it seemed something was slightly wrong, he didn't connect it with the bracelets, and didn't stop to examine the small doubt. The main thing was, Judy had come.

They walked briskly to the back where his car was. 'Nice,' Linda said softly. 'Very nice. I'm glad I came.'

'Good,' he approved, 'and how is it today? Frigid, or have you decided to stop being stuffy?'

51

Linda loved doing this. Many times before, she had neatly stepped into a promising friendship Judy was working up, and skilfully found out how far things had gone, and artistically put one small spanner in the works, so it was impossible afterwards for the man concerned to think just what had been done or said that had caused him to feel he didn't want to continue the alliance.

Now she knew just where they stood. 'A little ... less ... frigid perhaps,' she murmured. 'We'll see.'

'We'll see ... what?' he laughed, getting in beside her and slipping the engine into gear. Oddly with the triumph was the tiniest sense of disappointment. So Judy was no different after all.

He was a very skilful driver. 'Can you drive, Judy?' he asked her, and wasn't surprised when he got an affirmative answer. Judy would be efficient at most things, he thought.

'Want to take a turn at the wheel?' he asked a little later. He couldn't think why he had said that. Usually he didn't like anyone else to touch a car of his.

Linda said, 'Do you mean it?' in just the way Judy would, and when he let her take the wheel, she resisted the desire to open out at 80 or 90 – and kept to what Judy would consider fast enough; sixty on straight roads, and sedately through the towns. They went for a long drive, before finally putting up on a deserted coast road, at Richard's suggestion.

'Why have we stopped?' Linda asked, enjoying herself. It was not a question she would have chosen to ask, but one that Judy would undoubtedly have put to him.

'Are you sure you don't know?' he asked softly, taking her into his arms. He looked as if he expected a struggle, so Linda put up a faint-hearted one, and then said, 'All right, you win. I don't know why I bothered to say no the last time.'

Richard looked at her for a second, not quite knowing what to make of this. He had thought he had come to understand Judy very well in an extremely short time. It seemed he had been wrong and he didn't like that either.

'You've been putting me up, haven't you? All the time!' he said in a displeased voice.

'It was fun while it lasted,' Linda murmured.

She wondered why he looked at her so long, before he finally kissed her. For Judy it would have been an unpleasant, perhaps frightening way of kissing her but Linda liked it and rose to it, with enthusiasm. She liked her men-friends to be ardent and enthusiastic, but she also liked them to know when she was bored. Richard was out of his depth and looked it.

'Just what are you playing at, Judy? First you play at being frigid, all hurt, making me feel a perfect heel, and then you turn on, and now you're fed up. Just what *is* this?'

'Dear boy,' Linda sighed, 'do we have to stay on this windy coast road all the afternoon or do we have some tea somewhere?'

'Judy, I don't understand you at all!' he exclaimed. 'Take those damned glasses off and let me at least see your eyes. I can't make you out today at all.'

Linda put her hands up to hold the glasses in place. 'Don't touch them!' she said sharply. 'I'll get a headache if I don't keep them on! Oh, it's nothing – just the light too harsh. You a doctor and you haven't heard that people with dark eyes can't stand strong light?'

He didn't like that either, and turned round to the wheel. 'All right, if you're going to be in this quarrelsome mood, let's go and find some tea. I suppose I can't expect anything else with hair that colour!'

'What's wrong with my colour hair?' Linda flashed. It had always been a sore point with her.

'Redhead, sorehead, gingerbread,' Richard chanted, his good humour restored. He never stayed in a bad mood for long. He didn't expect Judy to, either. Linda shot him a look that left her lovely mouth sulky in the extreme. 'Funny,' he said, 'you didn't seem at all like this yesterday! I wouldn't have thought you could be so different one day and then be like this!'

Linda went quiet, her boredom evaporating. This was fun, finding out what Judy had done and said in private, on her day out with Richard. 'What was so special about me yesterday?' she flashed.

'Oh, I don't know,' Richard said uneasily, concentrating on entering the town from the comparative quiet of the coast road. 'You seemed rather gentle yesterday, nice somehow, kind, warm. Today you're just the reverse! Stop fooling with me, Judy I like the way you were yesterday.'

'But with the kissing of today thrown in, for good measure,' Linda said shrewdly.

He had the grace to laugh. 'Well, yes, that combination would be perfect!' he admitted.

'Well, a person can't have it all ways, can he?' Linda said softly. 'Or didn't they tell you that when you were a little boy? Are you just a grown-up spoilt brat?'

'That's me,' he said amiably. 'But now I've discovered how you can kiss, my love, when you take your back hair down, then there's going to be no more nonsense on that score!'

Linda merely smiled, and from behind her dark glasses she set out to be amusing, entertaining, but getting steadily more bored with his company until he regretfully took her back to the hospital. What, she asked herself, was so special about this Dr Cartwright? He was handsome, yes, but no more than an overgrown schoolboy, really, so sure that the world was his oyster because his father was wealthy. She had, she decided, met much more entertaining men among the older age group. She wondered idly what Philip Addison would turn out to be like.

Chapter Four

Thelma and Sheila were out when Linda got back. She found Judy alone in their room, tidying the drawers of her chest and turfing out some of Linda's things that had got in there.

'What's the idea, throwing my things out?' Linda asked indignantly.

'I'm not throwing them out,' Judy said in surprise. 'I'm putting them in your drawers.'

'Why? I haven't got room! I've always overflowed into your drawers. Stop it! I shall be gummed up with too many things.'

'I can't help it, Linda. It's a rule here. Nobody allowed to share other people's drawers and cupboards. Home Sister inspects. And she's pretty hot on guessing which belongs to which. Besides, it's a nice rule. I'm a bit tired of having your things jammed in with mine,' Judy said reasonably. 'You've got plenty of room.'

Linda decided not to push the point any further. 'Where are the other two?' she asked.

'Gone out in a foursome with the Casualty Officer and a boy called Douglas Knapp.'

'Oh, is he any good?' Linda was always

interested in other people's men-friends.

'He's the clumsy boy who adores Sheila,' Judy said quietly. 'He did very well with a one-man band thing today. He was very comical.'

'Oh, I know the oaf you mean,' Linda yawned. 'Poor Sheila!' She tore off her things and dropped them on the floor, as she had always done in the aunt's house, but Judy just stepped over them. 'What's the matter with you, Judy? Aren't you going to put my things away for me?' Linda asked in genuine surprise.

'I've been thinking about that,' Judy said, seriously. 'I know I did it for you in PTS, just like at home, only we had a room to ourselves there. Now we share with two other people.'

'So?' Linda asked sharply.

'Well, I wouldn't like them to see me putting your things away. They might think you were lazy. Well, it wouldn't be doing you a service, and besides, I think it's time we changed our ways – we're nurses now, not children, and I think we ought to be responsible people.'

Linda snapped her eyelids but kept her temper with an effort. 'All right, just as you say,' and she smiled sweetly at Judy, and picked her things up. As she folded them and put them in her own drawers she took advantage of Judy's pleased surprise by asking, innocently, 'What did you do today while I was out?'

Judy said, 'Oh, we had fun. We rehearsed, then one of the sisters wanted a poor chap in her ward to hear the bit of Rubenstein I'd been playing and in the end they took an upright piano in there and I played. Funny, I suppose nobody thought of it before. The patients liked it and want some more tomorrow.'

Linda's eyes widened. 'That's a cute trick on your part – I would never have thought of that! Golly, how many hours can you get off ward work while you play jolly tunes to the fellows?'

Judy looked momentarily put out. 'It's to be in my spare time,' she said.

'Oh,' Linda said flatly, and abandoned the subject.

'Lin, why did you go out after saying you'd sing at the rehearsal?'

'Well, you know me,' Linda said, sitting down and beginning to do her nails. The smell of varnish remover filled the room, hot from catching the sunshine all day long. She said, 'I just suddenly couldn't bear the thought of singing before all those people so ... I just went out. It was wonderful, escaping.'

'You went out by yourself?' Judy asked carefully.

'Now you know where I would have gone,'

Linda said reasonably as if Judy were being very difficult and stupid. 'I took my turn with Richard Cartwright. It's your turn next time.'

'But I'd told him I couldn't come!' Judy exclaimed.

'So? He just thought you'd altered your mind, I suppose.'

'You mean you let him think it was me?'

'We've done it before,' Linda shrugged. 'It wasn't difficult – I just kept my dark glasses on. It was too easy, if you want to know, and in the end it got rather boring.'

'Then you'd better tell me exactly what happened,' Judy said heatedly, 'because I shall look pretty silly next time I see him.'

'I wonder,' Linda said, and her smile was one of anticipation. Her eyes danced, but she merely said, 'I think on the whole that he'll like you best. He didn't make much headway with me. He's really rather a boy, isn't he?' and that was all Judy could get out of her. When Linda didn't want to talk, she had ways of stopping the conversation, and soon after that, the others came in, Sheila full of her wrath at the clumsiness of Douglas Knapp, who had somehow got it into his head that he only had to ask her, to get an engagement going. 'Who wants to be engaged to *him?*' she exploded. 'Judy, what can one do with a fellow like that?'

'He does like you rather a lot,' Judy said,

feeling sorry for Douglas, but wanting to be alone to think of Richard and herself, and of what could possibly have happened that day with Richard and Linda, that he hadn't even realised it wasn't Judy.

What, she asked herself, could Linda have done? A cold feeling swept through her, and she thought of other young men she had rather liked but who had never asked her out again after Linda had taken her place on a date.

After the other two had gone charging down the passage to the bathrooms, she turned to her cousin. 'Now we are nurses,' she began, 'I think it is rather a good time to change other things, such as sharing our boy-friends.'

She expected Linda to make a fuss, but Linda merely looked up in an amused way and said, 'All right, if you like.'

'You mean you won't mind?' Judy asked in perplexity. Really, Linda could be very tricky when she was in a bad mood.

'You've got what you want. Aren't you satisfied?' Linda said.

'I didn't expect you to agree to stop sharing men-friends, that's all,' Judy said.

'Let's establish which man you don't want, so I can consider having him,' Linda said, as if it were a very reasonable idea. 'I take it you don't want Richard?'

'What makes you say that?' Judy gasped.

'Oh, you do! Well, that's established, then. So you won't want Philip Addison? Well, they tell me he always goes out of his way to speak to you if he can find a chance and he's an older man so that seems a little sinister, doesn't it, considering we're only First Years?'

'Who said Mr Addison goes out of his way to speak to me? I have only encountered him once and that was when I dropped—' Judy began, but Linda made a gesture of impatience.

'So you don't want to admit anything! I merely said what I have heard. I heard a Staff Nurse saying to one of the other nurses on our ward that you were a bit of a menace because you look so innocent and Philip Addison looks all goo-ey at you.'

'I don't believe it!' Judy flared.

'And the women say he's very kind to you and smiles at you but never looks at any other nurse—'

'But it's not true!' Judy stammered.

'And I distinctly saw him look at you myself – well, to tell you the truth, after the women had said that, I made it my business to see if there were any truth in it, and there is, you know – he does look at you in rather a soppy way, but of course, if you don't want him, you've only got to say, and I'll have a shot at seeing if he's any good. I like an older man and they say he isn't hard up, but if he's boring, then I'll give him back to you,' Linda said kindly.

'What makes you so sure that you can just make any man ask you out, at the drop of a hat?' Judy fumed. This came up time and time again and she had to admit that Linda always seemed to have a new man-friend without any difficulty at all.

'Well, let's not argue about that,' Linda said sweetly. 'Especially as the others are coming. Let's agree you still want to keep little Richard, is that it? You have him, dear. He's a bit on the naive side for me!'

No more was said that night. Thelma and Sheila were full of themselves for having discovered two free bathrooms at the same time.

But Judy thought of what Linda had said about Philip Addison the next day when he came upon her unexpectedly in the dark end of the corridor where they kept the pots for the flowers brought for the patients. Judy couldn't get the old tap turned on. He glanced down the end as he passed, saw her predicament and came to help her.

Her face flamed. 'Oh, no sir, please don't – I mean, it'll be a messy job and I couldn't ask you–'

He took no notice of her protests and turned the tap on. 'It wants a new washer,' he said in a matter-of-fact voice. 'Do you know how to go about getting one? No? I thought not! You send down to the boiler-man in the basement.'

'Oh, yes, thank you,' Judy gasped. 'I know where! As a matter of fact, I can see him on the way to X-rays – I've got an errand as soon as I finish this.'

He smiled at her. He was a very tall man, not skinny like Bobby Jeeves, but well-built, and his face had the length and sad lines of a bloodhound, Judy found herself thinking. She wished he would go. He was too important to be discovered standing here talking to a little Green-Check, and she'd get into trouble. She pushed the flowers pell-mell into the pot, spilt the water down the front of herself and blushed a deeper red.

'Now you'll have to change your apron as well,' he remarked. 'Go on, take those into the ward and get your thing for X-rays and I'll walk you down. I can't have you getting lost.'

It was just as he said. Judy got sharp words from the ward sister for making a mess of her apron and was summarily dispatched to change it and to take her file down.

Philip Addison was talking to the Staff Nurse, earnestly regarding a paper of hand-writing she had given him. She was getting steamed up about something and Philip Addison was giving the matter his complete attention. Judy was so relieved. She scooted down the corridor and vanished round the corner thankfully.

He caught her up at the bottom of the stairs, and went on talking as if there had been no break at all. 'Taps are something in my line,' he said chattily. 'I thank my stars that my father insisted that we boys should all be useful at homely things. He used to say it was no use having sons if you had to engage outside help for simple things in the house.'

'How many brothers have you, sir?' Judy asked politely, but with interest, too. Suddenly she saw a rather funny mind picture of a line of boys, all with Philip Addison's tired bloodhound face, and a huge father with a horsewhip settling them down to change washers on taps.

'Three, and none of them looked a bit like me,' he said coolly, exploding her fanciful picture. 'And considering that my father was not a big man, he was something of a bully. Six inches shorter than I am,' he confided. 'Have you got any brothers?'

'No, I rather wish I had,' Judy said regretfully.

'Only this cousin of yours, who is so much like you.'

She was surprised that he knew there were two of them and that Richard didn't. But of course, Philip Addison was always on this ward, taking an outsize interest in everything. In fact, the ward sister had been known to explode with wrath every time he appeared on the scene. A good ward sister, she had been heard to say, is worth any doctor, and with much less fuss.

'Only my cousin,' Judy said evenly.

'No other family?' he pursued, and she agreed. 'Nobody else.'

'Then somebody ought to play the part of a big brother, don't you think, and warn you about our glamorous Dr Cartwright. Don't take him too seriously, will you?' And as her face flamed, this time with annoyance, he said, 'Now I've made you cross. It's only for your own good. You look such a nice little thing and already other ward sisters are saying how devoted you are, playing that old piano for the chaps, I hear. I don't think you're really fitted to fight for your own self.'

'It's very kind of you, sir,' she began, but with a broad smile, he said, 'Would you like to meet my brothers? They're all music mad,' which took the wind out of her sails and made her smile without meaning to. 'That's better!' he approved. 'One is a professor at the School of Music in Skidgate, and the other two just play at composing, and do the odd concert. Lazy lot, my brothers.' He looked to the right as he spoke, and pointed: 'Your way to the boilerman, I think. And let me know when you'd like to make Harold's acquaintance. The professor at Skidgate Academy of Music,' he explained as if he thought she hadn't been listening at all.

She had never felt hotter in her life. Telling the boilerman what she wanted and ensuring that it was done that day and not next week, finished her. She was stammering when she left him, but mainly because Linda, with her cool manner and a minimum of time and effort, had found out that Philip Addison was interested in Judy, when all the time Judy had been busy dreaming about Rick Cartwright.

She had met many men in her life, but none of them had made such an impact as Richard Cartwright and – in his special way – as Philip Addison. As Judy hurried over to the X-ray department, and then dashed back to her ward, she thought that Philip Addison might prove, in his way, to be just as upsetting, and that wasn't sense, really, she told herself, because he was so kindly, so friendly in a light sort of way that couldn't be objected to, and oddly he was always there just when she needed that special friendliness that he had to offer.

She decided she would keep out of his way. It was a purely defensive piece of reasoning, but Linda's observation had a lot to do with it. She didn't want Linda to make clever remarks about Philip Addison's attentions, however harmless they might be. Nor did she want Linda to probe into her feelings about Rick, which was not at all easy to understand, considering how close she and Linda had been all their lives. It was as if, in coming to this hospital and meeting Dr Cartwright, their firm relationship had been blasted apart, through neither Judy's nor Linda's efforts. Passionately Judy didn't want to lose that relationship with Linda. It was family, and all she had. They had their small fights and bore no umbrage; Linda rejected gently but firmly any show of affection but never rejected Judy's alliance, that close alliance that was made up of blood relationship and fierce loyalty. Linda never refused those, and Judy saw no reason why even Dr Cartwright should spoil things for her and Linda. She would, she told herself, rather lose Dr Cartwright than lose Linda. Linda's closeness was of a lifetime, and Rick Cartwright was too new to even understand.

With this in mind, Judy decided that she would accept Sheila and Thelma's tentative suggestion that they should all spend the next free day together, in the country. A picnic on someone's farm. Of course, Sheila was madly thrilled about it. She would go about sniffing the farm smells and being in seventh heaven, and would probably dissolve into tears when she got back to the Nurses' Home. But it would be a nice change.

Before that could happen, however, the

ward sister made herself happy by definitely splitting the cousins, and sending Linda to a male ward. Now she could breathe freely. She also promised herself that if Matron took on two girls again that even looked remotely alike, she would put in a special request not to have either of them on her ward. For the moment, however, she had a good bargain; she realised that as soon as Linda went. It was Judy the women liked. Unfortunately it was Judy that the men liked, and there were more students and doctors calling at that ward than there had ever been before, especially Philip Addison and Dr Cartwright.

'Proper honeypot, she is,' Mrs Pepping said fondly, 'and she don't even realise it! That's the beauty of it! I said to her that day that she *would* take me back to the ward and there was that Dr Cartwright waiting to chat her up, I said to her that he'd never been treated like that before by a little nurse, and to look out, but bless me, it don't seem to have made any difference. He's after her more than ever!'

The women discussed it avidly, and they weren't slow to see what Philip Addison's interest was. 'But of course, he's old for her,' Mrs Pepping pronounced. 'Wants a nice young man, she does!'

'Oh, I don't know,' Miss Ramage protested. 'He's very nice and he's only in his early thirties, and he's got a lot of money.'

'So have the Cartwrights,' everyone else said. 'And he's young and good-looking!'

'But flighty,' Miss Ramage pointed out. 'A flighty husband's no good, not for a nice girl like Nurse Blayne.'

'Well, there they both come,' one of the women murmured. 'So who is our Nurse Blayne out with today, I wonder?'

The farm to which the four girls had decided to go was an old-fashioned one. Some of its outbuildings looked as if they were about to collapse, but on closer inspection, this was an illusion.

'My father knows the farmer,' Sheila told them. 'An old patient. And I know this farm. But he's taken in some others in his family since I came here last. He's getting on a bit and without a lot of mechanical help, it *is* hard work. But oh, the smell of it – the lucky, lucky things to live here!'

'Thank heavens the sea is in sight,' Linda murmured, and turned her delicate nose in that direction.

'You really like all this?' A masculine voice cut in on their conversation, and made Sheila jump, so that she took a step backwards, ankle-deep in mellifluous mud. Linda began to laugh at Sheila's dismay but Judy said, 'Oh, Sheila, you can't manage like that all day! You'll have to take things off! Oh, what bad luck!'

The young man looked at both the redheads in turn, and said quietly, 'Come back to the house. My aunt will help you. I'm Victor Grant, by the way. The cousin from Lincolnshire, in case they ever mentioned me,' and his tanned face creased up at Sheila in a comical smile that was echoed by her. He was tall and strong in a lean muscly way. A strong young man for an outdoor job and he loved his work. That was obvious, the way he talked about it as he led them through the stackyard to the farmhouse. He loved the farm and the life, and Thelma murmured to Judy, 'Why did we come? She'll be wretched for days after this.'

The farmhouse had been four cottages, knocked into one. The conversion hadn't been very clever, but yet it had an accidental charm of its own. The ceilings were low, there were too many staircases, too many dark narrow passages. 'But we're getting down to doing something about it in the winter, my cousins and I,' Victor said engagingly, as he searched everywhere for his aunt.

The windows were small and filled with pot plants and there were lamps that needed pumping up, but electricity too. 'The generator gives out sometimes, so it's useful to have lamps,' Victor told them, pushing cats out of the way for the girls to sit in armchairs that were covered with throw-overs, made of wool patchwork. 'Throw-overs are coming back into fashion,' Judy murmured, smoothing them, while Victor went out to the dairy, yelling for Aunt Mary. Linda raised her elegant eyebrows and remarked that a lot of the stuff could usefully be thrown away, but the other three shouted her down.

'Oh, no, it's all in keeping! I love the fat cushions and the table covers–'

'Don't tell me that's a locked *Bible* on that side table! It *is* you know!' Sheila breathed in awe. '*And* an album of Edwardian actresses.'

'Well, there's certainly enough Victoriana here to fetch a lot of money,' Linda said smilingly, glad to be able to agree with something about a place she didn't like at all.

Victor came back with his aunt. Their weight shook the floor boards. Mrs Evans was shorter than her nephew but fat and heavy. She wheezed as she came but her face was one broad smile. The girls saw why they hadn't heard footfalls; both Victor and his aunt had discarded their boots at the back door. Sheila looked guiltily down at her soiled feet and the marks they had made on the stone floor, and she stammered apologies.

'Not to worry, love,' Mrs Evans said comfortably. 'The girl has a bucket of soapy water on the go this minute, and a few more bits of flooring won't hurt her. Come you to the bathroom,' and talking all the way, she bore them off to a really large bathroom that had once been a room, converted with the rest of the place. 'Now what's all this talk of picnicking in the woods, then? Nasty damp place this time of year. You just eat with us! Bless you, there's enough and more. We'll have it all snug in the parlour and leave the men in the kitchen, and you shall tell me all about what you young things get up to at the hospital in your spare time, with all them good looking young doctors, now!'

It was a wonderful day. Victor took them round the whole farm showing them things, but it was to Sheila that he talked, though at times his eyes wandered appreciatively towards the two redheads. But Sheila was the one who wanted to know about everything, and who could talk more knowledgeably about growing things, soil and humus, than she could at the hospital over her work there. Linda tactlessly said so, which made them all laugh.

Victor looked down at Sheila and said, 'Don't you like your work at the hospital, then?'

'I've got to like it,' Sheila said shortly, then, a wistful note creeping into her voice, 'but this is what I'd like to do. I suppose you don't want a landgirl or something?'

'You wouldn't like working on an inconvenient farm like this, out in all weathers,' he laughed, but he kept looking at her, considering.

Linda said, 'Another pair of shoes ruined,' and examined the soles of her good new leather walking shoes. 'Why didn't we think to come in gumboots?'

Judy said, 'Oh, it was worth it. I adore that farmhouse. The only place we haven't seen into yet is that end barn. What's in it?' she asked Victor.

'That's the last place, for a surprise,' he said, and when they crowded in, all that was to be seen in the dim warm darkness was a proud cat and her newish litter. He picked up one. 'Just got their eyes open today,' he said. 'I thought you'd like this little'n. You are a cat-lover, aren't you, Sheila?' he asked anxiously.

'Oh, yes, I am, I am, but I can't have it! It wouldn't be allowed in the Nurses' Home,' she wailed.

'Not to worry. We'll keep it here for you if you'd like it, then you'll have to keep coming back to see it.'

Linda backed out, murmuring about rustic love, but Judy hushed her. 'You leave him alone,' Judy said fiercely. 'It's the first time I've seen Sheila really happy since we first met her!'

'But she can't keep coming to this farm,' Linda said reasonably. 'Look at the trouble we took to reach here today and then only because we had a whole day off and the weather was fine. Think how she'd manage if it was pouring, or icy.'

'It might not appeal to you, but I daresay that young man would provide transport to come and fetch her if things went their way,' Judy said stoutly.

Linda started to laugh softly, and jeered, 'Matchmaker!' which made Judy laugh. They were both laughing when the others came out. Judy looked at Sheila and thought with surprise that that round fat happy-go-lucky face was suddenly almost pretty. Was that what love did to one? Was that what her turbulent feelings about Rick Cartwright did to her? She couldn't believe it. Her feelings were not of happiness overspilling, she thought with surprise. Her feelings were as if she had been taken up by a giant wave, and was being borne heaven knew where, and she was a little frightened about where she would land when that giant wave dashed her downwards.

This feeling persisted and she couldn't shake it off. It was still there when they returned to the hospital at the end of a day that had been interesting and relaxed, with swimming thrown in, and a walk through the really thick woods. It had been a lovely spot, nice people at the farm, good weather, and plenty to eat. Nurses are always hungry, Judy thought in surprise. She was also surprised to find that the others were all happy and relaxed but she wasn't, and she was taut as stretched elastic when she suddenly saw Rick. He was on one of the balconies, watching them coming in, talking and laughing. He turned away as if he were going to hurry down, cut them off as they went across the grass to the back of the Nurses' Home. Absurdly Judy wanted to hide. They had a head start of him. If only someone would catch him, hold him up, till they reached the Nurses' Home.

In the end, that is what happened. Judy thankfully followed the others upstairs, when the telephone rang. It was Rick, wrathfully demanding that she come out again, to speak to him. 'Meet me behind the Residents' Car Park,' he ordered, and surprised, she didn't attempt to refuse.

Linda came back. 'Rick?' she asked and seemed amused. 'Do tell me what happens – I mean to say, you look as if you're going to the guillotine, not to meet the man of the moment!'

Judy watched her cousin sauntering up the stairs, not a care in the world. Linda didn't want him, she couldn't possibly, Judy thought in swift relief. So then the field was clear for herself. They could take up where they left off, if that was what he wanted. She hurried to the car park.

He was marching up and down. The cars

and the wall hid him for the moment. Then he beckoned her, and they went behind the wall in the shadows. The sun didn't reach here and she shivered. 'Did you want me, Rick?' she asked.

He mimicked her. 'Of course I wanted you! You didn't tell me you were going out with a hen party! You agreed that you'd come to Oakmere with me. Why didn't you wait for me?'

She whitened. Was this what had amused Linda so much? Why hadn't Linda told her that was what had been arranged?

Before her anger could take hold of her, he pulled her to him and began kissing her, demandingly, savagely. It was seconds before she could free her bruised mouth from the demands of his.

'Don't! Don't ever do that again!' she stuttered furiously. 'I told you that, last time I was out with you! Don't you take *any* notice? Because if not, you can scrub any other dates with me!'

His eyebrows shot up but he looked angry, too, and bothered as if there was something here that he didn't understand at all. 'Well, I'm dashed! The last time you were out with me, indeed! Or have you forgotten how much you liked it then? Don't you play with me, Judy! I'm too experienced at the game. I might get rough.'

'I believe you would,' she said softly. 'But

just take it from me that I never in my life liked that sort of kissing, not from you or anyone!'

'Hey, don't walk away! You can't get away with that! Convincing as you are, I'm not going to have that! Good heavens, I could almost believe there were two of you, the way you're acting – it won't do, my girl! It won't do at all!'

She stood still, considering him. So this was what made Linda laugh softly to herself, all the way up the stairs. She had let him kiss her like that? Well, yes, she would, Judy had to allow, and she would think no more of it. Linda had no intention of going out with him again. She would get her fun out of making a fool of him, and of watching Judy's indignant face, recounting it. 'You just never kissed me like that before, Richard,' she said in a low tone. 'As for whether there are two of us,' she said, remembering Linda had worn dark glasses, 'the next time you think it's me, just take off the sun glasses, and use your eyes, will you?'

She looked back from the end of the passage, willing herself to look at his flushed angry face, but he had turned and was already striding away without a backward glance for her. Well, that would be another romance that Linda had had fun with, she told herself.

Briefly she transferred her anger to her

cousin, but it didn't last long. She was honest enough to remind herself that if it hadn't been Linda, it would have been some other girl. It wasn't Judy that Rick cared for, she told herself; it was the novelty of being refused, feeling aggrieved, because it had never happened to him before. He would get over it. There would be a long line of other girls. But meantime it hurt horribly in the place where her heart ought to be.

Linda looked up with that sweet smile on her face, as Judy went into their room in the Nurses' Home. Nobody would think that she had thrown such a spanner into the works. 'All right?' she even had the cheek to say.

'All right,' Judy said in a level tone, turning her attention to the vivid Sheila, still drooling over the wonderful day they had had at the farm.

Linda wouldn't let it rest. 'I forgot to tell you that he wanted to take you (or me) whichever, to his home today. Still, I'm sure we had more fun than we might have had.'

'Yes, I'm sure,' Judy allowed, still not looking at Linda.

'Was he cross?' Linda persisted.

'Predictably so,' Judy said, with a little smile.

'And ... nothing else happened?' Linda was now intrigued.

'Now what,' Judy asked reasonably, 'would

happen to *me?*' neatly inferring that it was to Linda that the exciting things happened. But of course, Linda knew better than that. There would have been a row because Judy wouldn't like to be kissed like that and Linda wanted to hear about it. And she wanted to know what had been arranged: that is, whether he could forgive them for making a fool of him, or whether he had selected one of the two of them for keeps. Or were they to have fun sharing him?

Judy briefly played with danger, refusing to confide in her cousin. It wouldn't do, of course. Linda knew she was holding something back. Linda wouldn't like that. She would repay in the same coin, and perhaps it would be something Judy wanted to know very badly that Linda would hold back. Judy worried about it for a few minutes, then abandoned it. Whichever way one looked at it, things weren't the same between them. Rick Cartwright had done that to them and he didn't even know.

Chapter Five

Bobby Jeeves was fascinated with the standard of Judy's piano playing, and with her generosity over free times. She gave up an outing with the other girls to play nursery rhymes and game songs on the old upright in the children's wing one afternoon, and because a man in the private ward heard about it and wanted to hear some classical music, Judy played to him in visiting time. He had nobody else that evening and it took his mind off his eyes, which were still bandaged, after his operation.

Bobby Jeeves still wanted Judy to attend rehearsals. 'You can't expect it,' Thelma exclaimed, as they were making up the lists. 'The poor girl never gets any time to herself!'

'Is she complaining?' he asked reasonably, but he and Thelma were on strained relations lately. Bobby wanted them to be married, and carry on their work. Nurses were so short nowadays that it would be allowed here, he insisted. Thelma wouldn't hear of it. 'It won't work and you know it – we shall find we're starting a family with no home and only your pay and I'd hate that!'

They had avoided an open quarrel so far,

but the matter of the cousins curiously brought it to a head and Thelma could never see afterwards how it had done. She could only suppose that it inevitably brought up the question of Linda's voice.

'Well, if Judy's so hard-pressed doing her stint on the piano for the patients, what's wrong with Linda singing for us, but no, we're not allowed to get a whisper from the million dollar voice!'

'Don't be bitter, Bobby. It's just that Linda doesn't put herself out like Judy does, for other people. I expect she'll sing for us one of these days.'

'When we go down on bended knees to beg her, I suppose. Well, I won't. And don't let me catch you begging her, Thel!'

'But you *wanted* her to sing for you a minute ago!'

'I did mention it, but there's always this hoo-ha about if she's got time or feels inclined, and I could see the way you were looking, and I can't stand that sort of girl. Give me Judy, any time.'

Unreasonably Thelma wanted to take the opposite side. Bobby who had such an even disposition, had been getting so fractious over their proposed engagement lately and she had lost sight of the fact that that was one subject that could change that young man so swiftly. She took Linda's side, though she couldn't have said why she was doing so. It wasn't that she liked Linda.

'I think you're being beastly, Bobby, and one of these days Linda will sing for you and then you'll see that a fine voice can't be used at any old time.'

'Who says she's got a fine voice, apart, of course, from the loyal Judy?' he was quick to point out.

'I don't see any reason to believe she hasn't,' Thelma snapped back, and now it was a question of fighting Bobby, not so much defending Linda. 'After all, a fine voice has to be looked after and some people won't sing in wet weather even.'

'Oh, and I suppose any old bod can bang about on the piano!' Bobby retorted, intent only on getting even with Thelma, without thinking actively now about Judy. 'Let me tell you that there are pianists who insure their hands for thousands of pounds because they're afraid of losing the use of them and not being able to play any more.'

'Don't be more absurd than it's your nature to be, Bobby Jeeves – that only happens when a person gets a living and is famous, being a pianist,' Thelma was quick to retort, but at the same time she shivered a little. She quietened down and said, in a funny little voice, 'Oh! why did we start talking about that! I feel sort of cold and queer. Do you suppose you can make things happen by just talking about them?'

Bobby said, 'No, of course not. Don't be absurd. And what are we quarrelling about, for heaven's sake?'

'I don't know,' she said miserably, and if they'd had a few more minutes, they'd have made it up. But into the deserted rehearsal room Linda strolled, and because she felt in the mood and very virtuous to be in and available while Judy was out for once, she offered to sing.

Thelma looked at her with loathing, and said she'd get the rest of the people together. Bobby brightened and said he'd play the piano for her, and when Thelma came back with some of the people rehearsing for the show, Bobby was looking helplessly up at Linda, not bothering to play, but just listening to a quite beautiful and rich voice.

The others were surprised, too. This was the effect Linda liked to get. Hold off from letting anyone hear her sing until the whole lot of them were fed-up with asking her, and suddenly let them hear what the famous voice was like, so they were astonished and feeling just a bit mean. It had happened several times before. Judy could have told them that, but she didn't hold it against Linda. It was just Linda's way. She could have told them Linda was used to people clamouring round her like these were now, telling her how marvellous her voice was, asking for more to be sung, wondering aloud why she didn't let more people hear her more often. And so on. Linda revelled in it.

Judy had her own problems just then. She had done what they had been warned not to do: undertaken a shopping chore for a patient. She had missed the bus into Skidgate, a town she didn't know, and wondered just how disappointed the patient would be, and if it would be worth telephoning the hospital to try and find Thelma, to ask her advice. A car pulled into the side and Philip Addison looked out and offered her a lift.

'Lucky I came along, if it's Skidgate you want,' he said, but it wasn't luck at all. He had shamelessly watched her go out, and he also knew where she was going and why. That patient had asked any number of people to go for this errand before now. He had at last found someone in Judy who would do it.

But Philip wasn't going to let Judy know that. He said, 'I suppose it's just the shops in Skidgate that you're after?' and she didn't question it. She said simply, 'I'm going to find a book on salmon fishing for that patient in the ward where I played the other day. It's not an easy book to find, but he says there's a very big bookshop in Skidgate. Is there?'

'There is.'

'Do you think there's a chance I'll find this book there?' she asked, with real anxiety in her voice.

'I think so, Judy, but I wouldn't if I were you,' he said.

'Why not? If it's going to make the patient happy–'

'Judy, he's not going to be able to do any more fishing, not of any kind,' Philip Addison said. He knew. He had operated on the man. 'So why raise his hopes?'

'Does he know that?' she asked, and when Philip shook his head, she said sturdily, 'Then why let him guess, by not getting the book for him? I shall try, anyway, and if I can't get it, I shall try writing to the publishers, or even seeing if someone has a second-hand copy. I happen to know there isn't one in the Library – I've already tried.'

'Why do you do so much for other people? Don't they give you enough study to eat up your spare time?' he smiled at her.

'It's interesting, going shopping for people. Like peeping at what people are borrowing from the Public Library. I like people. Oh, I expect I'm inquisitive, but it really is because I like people. Anyway, I shouldn't bother you with what I'm doing. I hope I'm not taking you out of your way, Mr Addison.'

'No, well, you see, I'm the same – I too, like people. I have heard the patients talking about you, and when you're as senior as I am, you get beyond bothering about what people will think of what you do in your spare time. If I feel like giving a lift to a little nurse and helping her go shopping (that's if she doesn't mind and isn't expecting Dr Cartwright to meet her anywhere!) then I do it. That answer the question in those big dark eyes?'

She nodded. 'Oh, well, that's all right. I'm not afraid of getting into trouble myself being seen in a surgeon's car–'

'Oh, I'm so glad!'

'–but it did occur to me that people might think it odd of the surgeon to keep being seen with me and helping me and all that.'

'Well, as I say, I'm too old to care. I ought to have been an uncle, you know,' he confided. 'I'd have made a very good one, they tell me. Only my lazy brothers won't bother to marry and oblige me by producing nieces and nephews. It really is a shame!'

'Now you're laughing at me, sir.'

'Well, I will, if you don't stop calling me "sir" – at least while we're out of the hospital and in mufti. In these democratic days–' but she drowned his words by choking with laughter.

'I'm sorry, I always laugh when people say that. I don't know why? I expect it's because I don't believe that things are any different today. I know some people call their bosses by their first names without blinking, but I always have the feeling something's a bit odd – you know, like shortage of staff, not because the bosses like such easy-going habits.'

'No, well, I will make a confession. I do feel that if your cousin Linda or any of your pals started calling me Philip, I wouldn't like it overmuch and I might say so pretty smartly, but if you did it, I might think it rather cute. That just shows you what a born uncle I am, making favourites. All uncles unfairly favour one and kick the rest. So you see?'

He helped her find the book, battled with the shop assistant for a copy without a blemish and triumphantly bore her off to tea at a rather expensive hotel. After that, he said, 'Now this is what I want to suggest. You're going to have some rough times in hospital. Rough times with staff, patients, patients' relatives, and with your own friends, of both sexes. Now I want you to promise me that you'll come straight to me with any problem you might have, and we'll thrash it out and get it put right. Agreed?'

'Why?' she asked bluntly.

'You haven't been listening. Because it would give me pleasure – I'm going to take you along to meet my brother Harold and he's going to be livid that I've found a pianist before he did. He thinks he's the only one to find the treasures, you see.'

Judy enjoyed the time spent at the Skidgate Academy of Music. It was just a house, too large for people to want to live in nowadays, but that made it rather cosy. The usual muddle of musical sounds made nice discord; Judy beamed but Philip Addison screwed his face up and muttered something like, 'How awful!' and then they were taken to his brother's study. And as he had said, Harold was not at all like him.

He was slimly built thought just as tall as Philip, neater features, a thin elegant nose and a neatly trimmed dark beard and moustaches. Just as a principal of a music school ought to look, Judy thought.

They made her try the beautiful grand piano in the corner but Judy didn't play as well today. She was nervous, a little bothered about why Philip Addison should also disturb her. He and Richard. Not this other Addison, this Harold of the elegant ways and the appreciating eyes, that took in her glorious colouring and the sympathetic way her fingers moved over the keys. Here was no genius but a girl who loved music and played very well. Harold thought, on hearing that she was a nurse, that she might be a very good nurse. He decided he'd like to have her nurse him. There was that quality of warmth and cosiness about her, and he found himself thinking that the only thing about her that didn't blend was her red hair. He felt she ought to have had brown hair, a warm brown the shade of autumn leaves before they turned gold. Funny, that. And turning suddenly he saw the way his brother Philip was looking at her, before Philip quickly curtained his eyes. That really did surprise Harold.

Judy enjoyed that visit so much that she said so, and both the men were delighted. 'Isn't it nice,' Harold murmured to Philip over Judy's head, 'to find a young person these days who can say she's enjoyed herself, without feeling she is losing her trendiness?'

'Well, poor old fellow!' Philip gently jeered, but he knew what his brother meant, and nodded at him. Judy said in surprise, 'But I always say if I've enjoyed myself!'

'I know,' Philip agreed, 'but some girls don't. There are some nurses I could mention, that cousin of yours, too, I should think! At least, I am almost quoting the ward sister–'

Judy missed the twinkle in his eye and said crossly, 'Oh, why does everyone get at poor Linda? She's a very nice person!'

'Then why does she keep it a secret?' Philip retorted. 'You should hear the patients on the subject!'

His brother said quietly, 'Come again, Judy? I'd like you to, very much. Ask my brother to bring you.'

Friends, and the warmth of them, Judy thought, as they briskly left the Academy of Music and went to find Philip's car. How nice it all was. At that moment, with the hurt of Richard pushed well to the back of her mind, she was really happy. She told Philip how she felt. 'And I would really like to go there again if it isn't too much trouble.'

He didn't think that was worth answering. His own heart was almost singing, and he hadn't even noticed the way Harold had looked at him.

Judy said, 'Do you play the piano, sir?'

'Philip,' he automatically corrected, but he was thinking of their all male family at home and wondering what it would be like to have somebody like Judy around. It wasn't that she did anything scintillating, or made any effort to be witty. It was just that her personality filled everywhere, so that when she wasn't around, one missed her so – another thing he had heard the women on her ward say, and found himself heartily agreeing with them. 'No, I don't play. I am absolutely non-musical and don't ask me how come. I haven't an idea,' he grinned.

'Oh, I thought you might have some talent. You should hear my cousin Linda sing!' She said it with such simple pride, but it flicked him on the raw. Yes, he could take Judy to his home and charm his other two brothers and his father, but then Linda would want to come, and then there would be trouble. Philip hadn't been in hospital for most of his life without being able to spot the Lindas, with all their charm and their capacity for stirring things up, and too, he suspected, in this case, an abnormal desire to have what the other person had. Linda, he knew instinctively, would not want Judy to have anything that she couldn't help herself to if need be, or even spoil if she felt like it.

'Judy,' he said, as he drove her back, 'Are you specially keen on Richard Cartwright? Really keen, I mean? You'd mind if someone else cut in, I mean?'

She was at once on the defensive. 'Why do you ask? Katie Sutcliffe is always talking like that! Who else would want to butt in on what is just a casual friendship? I mean, I don't mind if my cousin goes out with him.'

'You really mean that?' he asked keenly.

'I don't want to talk about it,' she said.

'All right. There's another thing I want to ask you. What is your cousin Linda doing at this moment. Well, people talk about you two as if you were twins, and there's some devilry going on, about fooling Cartwright that there's only one of you. Word is going around and there's a lot of amusement about it, and he won't like it when he finds out, if you've both been playing a trick on him.'

She didn't answer. The ache was back there again. She wished he hadn't mentioned Richard, just when she was enjoying herself so much.

Philip went on, 'Of course, Cartwright is a tricky customer and it could be that he's pretending to be fooled by you two. I would feel happier if–'

'If what, Philip,' she said, without thinking.

After a silence, he said, 'Say that again.'

She reddened. 'There, I knew you wouldn't like it if I did as you said and used your Christian name. Why did you?'

'Bless me, I did like it! Funny thing, I've never thought much of my name, but it really sounded a jolly nice name, the way you said it!'

'Oh, now I know you're just teasing me,' she said. 'And as to Richard, it really doesn't matter. He'll sort everything out. Don't you worry about me.'

A chill wind sprang up, and there was a chill in the atmosphere between them, too. Something had left it with the mention of Dr Cartwright, and Philip could have kicked himself for doing so. Cartwright was very much his junior and there was really no need for him to feel so irritated about Cartwright. The lad was too wealthy, too spoiled, but he might shape up into a doctor yet, if the right young woman took him in hand. But it didn't have to be Judy, did it?

He asked her to let him take her into Jennets Cross the next day, but she refused. A little too quickly, which puzzled him. 'I can't think why you should hate the idea so much, or is it because you're cross with me?' he asked in surprise.

'No. No, I'm not cross, of course I'm not! It's just that, well, Richard took me to Jennets Cross. Do you know who owns Magnus Island, by the way?' She didn't know what made her ask, except that it had nagged at her, the way Richard had spoken of the ownership, and the easy way he had gone there, as if the place had been his own.

'Oh, that place! We do – my family, I mean. Why?'

'*You* do?' It was such a surprise, she didn't know what to say. 'And are you thinking of selling it?' she asked faintly.

'No, we are not,' he said abruptly, his thoughts elsewhere.

So Richard had lied to her. But why? The way people spoke, he must be rich enough to buy any island. But of course, if it was that island he wanted particularly and Philip's family would not sell to him, that perhaps explained his odd manner. She now had to rush to cover up. 'Well, it was just a thought. I always ask who owns islands. I think it must be rather interesting to own an island. Lovely to get away from it all, to escape.'

She was talking nonsense, to cover up, and he was looking oddly at her, and she was glad when they arrived at the Nurses' Home. She escaped before he could arrange to take her out some other day.

Now she wanted to see Richard, to ask him about that. She couldn't let it run on, knowing he could lie to her. But then, it was in keeping with the whole thing, wasn't it? Richard wasn't being serious about anything at all; merely amusing himself, while she was breaking her heart over him.

Sickened and ashamed at the way her innermost thoughts were running, she absently agreed to do another duty the following day – a duty that would, she supposed afterwards, force her to be unable to see Richard. Give her time to sort things out in her mind. Linda was amazed that she would give up any free time in such a way, but then Linda had always insisted on her rights.

'You'll make it bad for the rest of us if you take on extra things,' Linda scolded. 'Goodness, we're new. We're not supposed to do extra time.'

'It's just giving up half a day,' Judy said. 'And it's only helping out on Joseph's Ward. Cutting bread and butter, things like that, because they're a junior short. Besides, I don't mind.'

Linda gave it up. She had nothing to do, and they had been going to Jennets Cross shopping, but she supposed she could find someone else to go with. She should be doing the notes of that lecture, she frowned, but it was too beautiful a day for that.

She stepped it out along the quiet roads beyond the hospital and when a familiar car tooted behind her and pulled in, she grinned in a friendly way and paused while the door opened.

Richard wasn't exactly pleased. 'Judy, what the deuce are you doing, walking on your own when I'm supposed to be taking you out?' he demanded.

She said, making her voice so like Judy's that she herself was pleased with the effort, 'Stop scolding me and let me get in. I'd love to take the weight off my feet!'

He leaned over and shut her door, and looked at her but decided not to take the matter up here, so near the hospital. He drove to Jennets Cross and parked on the coast road again. It was quiet here and they could see for miles and be sure of no interruption. 'Now then,' he said, turning to her. But before he spoke, he remembered what Judy had said that last time and he put up a hand to pull off the sun glasses. He did it too quickly for Linda to stop him. It took her by surprise.

It took him by surprise, too. Linda's eyes were a light brown, flecked with green, as different from Judy's as any eyes could be. He just sat there and stared at her.

'Well, well, well, so now that bit of fun's over,' Linda smiled, and put her arm round his neck to pull his head down so that her mouth could reach his.

'Just a minute,' Rick said, flushing. 'You're not Judy!'

Linda murmured, 'Not Judy,' and raised her mouth to his and kissed him. 'Not Judy at all. Do you mind?'

Rick held that every girl kissed differently. He was an expert on the subject. He said, with a muted anger, 'Not Judy last time, either?' and Linda agreed.

'Darling Rick, you look quite put out! Now let me guess why? Fretting for Judy? Oh, hardly, come now! Afraid you've been made a fool of? Think I told all the others about this and they are now roaring their heads off with laughter? Ah, I thought so! Darling Rick, this is our little secret. I can assure you the others in our set have far too many problems of their own to care whether it is Judy or Linda being dated by dear Dr Cartwright.'

'But why, why?' he asked, putting her away from him, and glaring at her. He wanted Judy, not this girl and he didn't understand why he should. He had always liked a girl who kissed with some enjoyment, and this girl certainly did. It was Judy's frigid approach to that part of their friendship which had irked and irritated him so much. So why should he feel like this now?

Chapter Six

Linda stretched her arms above her head and looked luxurious. 'Oh, I don't know. We always do everything together. Boy-friends too,' she said, smiling broadly at his dismay.

'Do you! Then this one isn't going to be on the list! I've never heard of anything so disgusting! Good heavens, you compare notes, both of you.'

'Don't be silly, darling,' Linda yawned. 'I might, but I don't think, on consideration, that I would. Judy certainly would not. I found out how far you'd both got by the way you answered me. You've no idea how much you give away.'

'Well, what do you want, for heaven's sake?' And because she was still laughing at him, he took her roughly in his arms and kissed her until she was breathless.

'My, my, you are put out about it,' she murmured, when they came up for air. 'You know, that's a very *young* way to go on, Rick darling. Personally I like a man to be a little more suave, to hide his feelings a little more. It's rather boring to know exactly what's going on in his mind, especially when he feels a fool.'

Rick sat back and smoothed his hair. 'If you must know,' he said between his teeth, 'I had the idea from the first that there were two of you but I asked Judy and she said no.'

'She did?' Linda looked genuinely astonished.

No, Rick thought, Judy wouldn't lie. He had the grace to try and remember what he had asked her, and remembering those questions, she told the truth, the bare truth; that she wasn't a twin, that she hadn't a sister. But she might have been fair and told him her cousin was so much like her!

'No. She didn't,' he corrected himself shortly. 'Well, you are out with me. What shall we do?'

'Dear Rick, no fellow talks to me like that,' Linda breathed. 'You can drop me in Jennetts Cross, and I'll go shopping and have some tea and I'll take a taxi back to the hospital.'

He didn't like being dismissed like that, either. 'And what am I supposed to do?'

'You're almost but not quite snarling at me,' she smiled. 'I don't know. Go back for Judy, I expect. I think you like her more than you know, and that really isn't your line, is it? I suppose you'll be kicking yourself for falling in love with someone so frigid, soon.' She watched his face and knew she was near the mark. She was astonished, and didn't like that one bit.

'Whether I'm in love with Judy or not

hardly concerns you, Linda,' he said tautly, but all the time he was battling with his own feelings and hating Linda for being so shrewd. Of course it wasn't his style! What was he thinking about, to fall deeply in love with a First Year Nurse, at his own hospital? What an entanglement! What sort of idiot had he suddenly become?

Linda fumed silently, and just had to hit back somewhere, at someone, so she took the first point she could think of, to harm Judy. 'You know of course, that her hair isn't really red?' she told him. 'It was a bit of a giggle, and it fooled no end of fellows, but her own hair is mouse colour.'

'And she's so attached to you!' he marvelled. 'Really, someone ought to open that girl's eyes, as to what you're really like! For two pins I'd do it myself!'

'Please yourself,' she shrugged. 'But I wouldn't if I were you! She'll dislike you for running me down. Some people,' she told him, with rare insight, 'are so loyal, it's their undoing – they'd put their heads in the fire for the sake of loyalty. Judy's like that. She won't have anything said against me!'

And that was going to be the trouble. He took her to Jennetts Cross after all. Being Rick, he could disguise his feelings and be a pleasant, even gay companion. Linda studied him and wondered if she'd been wrong about him liking Judy so much. But she could sense that there was a point, now, to which he would reach and go no further. The interest he was nurturing, was not for her.

She seethed. It had never happened to her before, certainly not with a gay young man like this one. She wouldn't have minded so much if it had been an older man, a less popular one, but to think that Judy, of all people, should have captivated this man, and that she, Linda, couldn't move him, was too much. All of a sudden she wanted him, and she knew that if she couldn't take him from Judy she would keep on worrying at it, until she at least spoilt everything for Judy. Judy was the person most close to her but the one she had a tendency to hurt most, when she herself had suffered a set-back.

Judy was resting her feet on the end of the bed when she got back. The others were rushing in and out. Sometimes even the quiet Thelma went a little giddy and be-haved like a schoolgirl, Linda thought, as she bundled them both out and shut the door on them.

'It's their room too,' Judy objected, but not with very much energy. Her good nature had led her to do just a bit too much today, she thought, and wondered when her feet would stop throbbing.

'Never mind that,' Linda said shortly. 'Just what did you say to Rick Cartwright, the last time you saw him?'

Judy kept perfectly still, and stared at the ceiling, but she said quietly enough, 'Why?'

'Never mind why – what did you say to him?'

Judy looked at her cousin then. 'Have you been out with him today?'

Linda shrugged. 'I went out by myself. I had shopping to do at Jennetts Cross. He was in his car and picked me up – I was glad of the lift. But the thing is, he insisted on thinking it was you, so just for fun, I didn't disillusion him.'

'You wanted to play it that way,' Judy said slowly, 'so I didn't tell him I had a cousin who looked like me, though how on earth he didn't find out before now, I can't think. Everyone else seems to know, and does it matter, anyway?'

'Well, yes, it does, because he insisted on taking off my sun glasses and then he saw it wasn't you, and he was so mad! Really, that fellow's ego must be enormous! He's quite sure that I was coming pelting back to tell everyone about it, and that all the nurses would be agog to hear how he took it! I soon told him nobody cared about him that much to bother.'

'So that's all right,' Judy said at last, lying back again.

'Is that all you've got to say about it?'

'Lin, why are you so indignant? Or is it that you had a disappointing day? I'm sorry if you did, but don't take it out of me – I don't think I could bear it! I'm tired out!'

'Serves you right!' Linda retorted. 'I told you what it would be like if you made yourself so free with extra duties. It's bad for the rest of us, too.'

'Go and put some records on or something, and leave me in peace,' Judy begged.

'But I haven't finished discussing this yet,' Linda objected. 'It's a silly business, anyway, this both pretending to be each other.'

Judy rolled her head round to look at her cousin. It was a point that should be taken up, she supposed; she never tried to look like Linda, and the game had been Linda's idea from the first. But she couldn't be bothered to fight. Instead, she agreed, and said, 'I was going to suggest to you that we stopped it. Let's do that.'

'How do you mean?' Linda asked, suspicious at once.

'I'll dye my hair back again. I'm quite sure red hair doesn't really suit me. Everyone says so because I blush easily; and while we're on the subject, I think we'd better stop dressing alike. It's a bit awkward now, because our tastes aren't the same any more.'

Linda considered this. 'All right, yes, I agree. Okay. You had better take all my clothes – use the lot. I'll get a new outfit, that would be rather fun. And I vote we drop that drip Richard Cartwright – he thinks too much of himself altogether.'

Again Judy considered her cousin but decided not to take the point up.

'You do just as you like, Lin,' she said, closing her eyes, and meaning that if her cousin didn't want Richard any more, then Judy could be friends with him without the awkwardness that had existed so far. It would be rather nice, she thought.

Linda made herself plain at once. 'Well, what I would like is for both of us to drop him, like a hot coal. He's no good. Let the other soppy nurses chase him. No, I think we'd better have a shot at someone a bit more mature. Philip Addison, for instance – yes, I think that might be rather nice. Don't change your hair just yet, Judy. We might have some fun in that quarter.'

Judy shot up into a sitting position, her fatigue forgotten, hot words coming to her lips. Really, at times, Linda was the end! But Thelma and Sheila bounced in again, and the time for a quiet conversation was over. Judy lay down on the bed and closed her eyes. Well, what was the matter with her, wanting to hold on to Philip's nice big-brother friendship and have Rick Cartwright as her special friend as well? Since when had she, Judy, been the sort of girl to hog two men and try to keep her cousin out? She was shocked at herself.

But she was so tired of that red hair, she

really was glad of the chance to get rid of it. She had a half day the next day and decided to go into Skidgate, to a rather nice hairdressers she had seen there, and to have her hair cut really short and made the brown she had always had. There was just enough of the original colour showing at the roots to be a guide. She was considerably put out when Richard came running after her across the front turf of the hospital, calling her name.

'Judy!' and he was quite sure it was her.

She turned and waited for him.

'I know it's you! I know how to distinguish you both now,' he said, but he looked at her eyes before he smiled broadly. 'Yes, it's my girl! Come on. I'm fed up with the hospital today. Where are you off to, anyway?'

She told him, briefly, and with no great welcome for his presence.

'Well, that's all right. I'm pretty well up in things like that – I know a very good hairdresser. But must you have it cut short? Go blonde or something but don't cut it. I like long hair.'

'No, Richard. Just for once I'm going to have my hair the way I like it – the original brown, and very short,' she smiled, so he sketched a salute, but insisted on driving her there and waiting for her, and taking her to tea afterwards.

'How do I look?' she asked. This was to be

the test. She was sure she would know if he looked disappointed or disinterested.

'But that's nice!' he exclaimed in surprise. 'A jolly nice brown, too. Keep it that shade – it suits you!'

'Well, it ought to. It was always like that before Linda made me change it to be like her,' she laughed.

He almost blurted out that Linda had said it was 'mouse'. Really, that girl, he fumed!

After tea, he said, 'I want to talk to you, Judy. It's got to be now, too, while I'm in the mood. It's about your cousin.'

'Then we're not going to talk at all,' Judy said firmly.

'Yes, do let's. Let's walk on the beach. I don't much like sand in my shoes, but at least we can get away from the crowds. Thank heavens I brought you to Jennetts Cross instead of Skidgate. What on earth is so special about Skidgate, by the way?'

Not for worlds would she tell him that she had been taken by Philip to the Music School there. She said briefly, 'Big shops.'

'But not such good ones,' the worldly Richard said. But he steered her down the slope by the old harbour, and on to the deserted stretch of beach that led towards Magnus Island.

That was a mistake. Judy kept thinking of her accidentally stumbling on the knowledge that it belonged to Philip's family and that

Richard had misled her, at the very least.

'Look, Judy, I don't know how to say this. Has your Linda said anything about what we talked about, or did, when she was out with me?'

Judy shook her head. 'Only the bit about you being cross because you thought it was me. I can't help that. You should have known me by my manner. But it's partly because I'm fed up with that situation that I've had my hair done like me. And I'm not going to dress like Linda any more.'

'I say, you girls haven't fallen out because of me, have you? I wouldn't like that, you know!' he said sincerely.

She was absurdly pleased. 'No, Richard, we haven't fallen out. I wouldn't let that happen, not for anyone. Lin's all the family I've got. And even if she isn't my sister, we were brought up just as closely. I can't remember a time when she wasn't there, so you see?'

His mouth turned down. 'Well, what's going to happen if you marry? Surely she won't hang around, upsetting everything?'

'Of course she won't!'

'Oh, help, now I've made you angry! I didn't mean to. I'll take it back! Look, Judy, don't let's fight – this is too serious a conversation. Look, you know what I'm like about girls–'

'I know! You told me! Everyone's No. 1

Pin-Up Boy!'

'Yes, well it isn't like that where you're concerned.'

She stopped and whirled round on him. 'You are not to make fun of such a thing! I know I let it out that I was rather keen on you but I told you at the time – don't let it bother you. We're just friends, you and me, and when you're fed up with it, then you can take some other girl out. Understood?'

'But that's what I'm trying to tell you! I don't want to! Judy, look–'

She backed away from him. 'Richard, if you dare start about wanting to kiss me again, I'll – I'll kick you, I promise!'

'Oh, Judy, don't make me laugh at a time like this,' he begged. 'Can't you see what I'm trying to tell you? If it hadn't been for your Linda messing about, I wouldn't have known that I'm so keen on you. It's different, Judy, from the rest.'

'You mean,' she said, after a silence, 'that you want to marry me?'

'Oh, now look here, I'm not the marrying kind, m'dear. I've told you that before now, now haven't I?'

'Then what's all this about?' she stormed. 'You must be an awful clot, Dr Cartwright, if you don't know by now that I'm simply not interested in anything else!'

She turned and started to run, but the shingle was so loose and slippery, that she was over and flat on her face before she could do anything about it.

He lifted her up as easily as if she were a child, and set her on her feet, but he wouldn't let her go. 'All right,' he murmured, 'so help me, if it's the only way I can get you, all right, then I'll even say I'll marry you!'

After a long astonished look, Judy said, 'No! No, I can't have it like that– I won't! It isn't right. It's something to do with what happened between you and Linda!'

'It is *not!* Good heavens, what *do* you want, Judy?'

'Have you ever proposed to anyone before, Richard?' she said.

'Why do you want to know that?'

'It will help what I have to say to you.'

'All right, then, I haven't.' Surly about it now, he looked down at her, and wondered why he had had to have it shown him how he felt about Judy, by that tiresome Linda. He didn't like it.

Judy said, 'You see, you're being driven to say it, and that won't work, afterwards, I mean. Let's be reasonable, Richard – I've been hurt so much in my life, and I won't be hurt over a man I am to marry.'

'Well, how *can* you be? Goodness, I'd protect you against everybody! I'm like that – possessive about what belongs to me!' and now he was cheerful again and grinning. 'Judy, love, for pity's sake let me kiss you so

110

we can walk on. Talk while we're walking,' and he bent his head before she could argue any more.

This was not like kissing Linda at all. Kissing Judy told you what she was feeling, he thought, and he was rather dizzy himself when he finally lifted his head and looked at her.

Tears were like beads on the ends of her long lashes. 'I do so wish you wouldn't be in such a hurry to do that,' she whispered. 'Don't you understand that kissing is a very small part of being in love? It's nice, maybe, but not all that important!'

'Oh, *isn't* it!' he retorted. 'Let me tell you a chap can tell if he's going to like a girl from the way she kisses, and you, my love, now you've been brought to the point of kissing me without wanting to harm my delicate shins, are tops at it! I'm satisfied,' he said, tucking her hand in his arm, 'so now we can walk and talk.'

'Can we!' she said fiercely. 'Oh, you make me so cross! Anyone would think that all you had to do was to propose and kiss me and then everything's settled up for life!'

'That's right!' he agreed cheerfully. 'The two most important things! Well, what else is there? I've got a nice family and lashings of money – I don't even have to work in the hospital if I don't want to – and we also like each other and we can have fun, lots of fun!

I'm willing to take a bet, old girl, that you have personally had very little fun in your life. Linda maybe – that girl would get fun if she had to trample on every other girl in sight – but you, no!'

Judy tore her hand from his arm. 'Well, that's fine for a start! If you think we can have a marriage and you make remarks like that about Linda, then that's the first and biggest stumbling block!'

'Oh, help, yes, I forgot! I'll be kind to Linda, on my honour I will, love, only stop looking as if you're going to bite me, please!'

'It doesn't begin and end there, Rick,' she said desperately.

'Well, what else have I said?'

They stood leaning on the rails, looking down into the water. It was green today, with a lot of froth on the edge of it, and it smacked up at them, pounding on the old sea wall. 'Stand back,' Rick said protectively. 'You'll be soaked through!'

'It doesn't matter. Well, I like sea spray and wind on my face,' Judy said impatiently. 'Listen, Rick. You don't seem to realise what you've outlined as your ideal of living. You say that you've so much money that you don't have to go to work – what do your parents think about that attitude? And how could I respect a husband who didn't want to work? And I suppose you'd protest if I wanted to finish my training – yes, there you are, see! You just didn't think I might want to, did you?'

'Well, of course you didn't! Well, you couldn't, anyway, Judy – how could you, as my wife? Well, even if they do stretch a point and keep on married women, my wife couldn't!'

'There you are!' she said again. 'And when it comes to respect, there's another thing I can't respect you for, only you even forgot to mention it.'

'Now look, love, lots of fellows go out with other girls when they're married. It doesn't mean a thing! Some wives like the system.'

Judy flushed deeply. She hadn't even thought of that aspect. 'That rather settles it then, doesn't it, though that wasn't what I was thinking about.'

Now he was intrigued. 'What *was* eating you, then?'

'What you said about Magnus Island,' she said surprisingly.

'Magnus Island? What on earth are you talking about?'

'You said you often go on it because you're more or less expecting to own it! Well, that's the impression you gave me but it's not like that at all! It belongs to Philip Addison's family and they wouldn't dream of selling it!'

'Now look here,' Richard said angrily, 'have you been telling him–'

'No, I haven't. I wouldn't. I merely asked him, in passing, if he knew who owned the place, and he said his family did and I asked if they were going to sell it and he said no. He said it very definitely, and that was all that was said.'

Judy's weary tone convinced him more than any protestation. His face cleared. 'Oh, then it's all right. You've got it all wrong, anyway. It's nothing to do with you or me or Addison, for that matter. It's a long-standing thing between his guvnor and mine. I don't think they want the island so much as to quarrel over the possession of it. Anyway, why bring that up?'

'Because you didn't tell me the truth and I'd never be able to trust you again,' she said, leaving the rail and marching back to the sand.

'Oh, Judy, don't be silly – you love me! I know you do, by the way you kissed me! I tell you what – it's Addison mixing it for me! Have you been out with him?'

'You have no right to ask me that, Richard,' she said.

'Oh, haven't I! I've asked you to marry me!' he said indignantly.

'But I didn't accept you, and please, Richard, let's forget about it,' she begged, in such a tone that even he had the sense to leave the subject alone.

But he was so much put out about it that

he had to find Linda and have it out with her. It was Linda's fault: it must be. Judy would never go on like that, he was sure, if Linda hadn't been mischief-making.

When he found Linda, she, too, was incensed. Everyone was taking a new interest in Judy because of her hair. Remarks like, 'Are you one of those two red-headed nurses? Twins, we all thought you were,' was all very well, but when remarks like, 'It suits you, dear. Nice! Much better than that red hair! You be yourself – don't try to be like your cousin!' were made, Linda writhed. Judy's popularity had become a living thing to torment her.

So when Richard came up to her without preamble and said, 'What the devil have you been saying to Judy to upset her?' it was the last straw.

'I haven't said a word, little boy,' she murmured aggravatingly. 'And what makes you think I'd tell you what I talk to my own cousin about?'

'Because I happen to want to marry her and I don't want you messing our lives up, that's why! So let's have it understood now, shall we?'

When Linda was shocked or annoyed, she whitened. Her skin was like alabaster now, and her eyes seemed to darken a little. 'Tell me, when's the engagement?' she murmured.

'It isn't settled, and don't broadcast it –

Judy doesn't want everyone to know,' he snapped, wishing he had said nothing. He hadn't got the information he wanted, and as Judy had told him not long ago, he didn't stick to the truth if it didn't suit him. 'You do understand me – I mean that! If you put it around I shall deny it and that will be rotten for Judy!' he insisted.

For reasons of her own, Linda brightened, smiled nicely at him and said, 'All right. I agree. I won't say a word. Bully for you and Judy!' and she went swinging off, this time not imitating Judy's walk. Linda's walk had a touch of devilry in it. She was an unknown quantity. That agreement of her's worried him more than if she had made no promise at all.

Chapter Seven

Judy avoided Rick where possible, which wasn't difficult; as an expert avoider of work, Rick took a lot of beating.

So far as she knew, Judy supposed Linda was seeing him, but Sheila rather exploded this idea.

'Katie's been lent to Joseph Ward and she says there's a chappie there who's keen on your Linda, and your Linda is really very nice to him!'

It didn't bother Judy. Linda was always nice to men when she felt like it. 'What's he in for? Anything interesting?' she asked.

'He got some complicated bug out East which has made him go deaf in one ear and they think the other's going. Query op. but apparently there isn't much hope. He's crazy about opera so that may be the pull with your Linda,' Sheila said. 'My friend Victor Grant thinks–' and she broke off to flush brick red. Too many times nowadays, since that visit to that farm, Sheila mentioned that young man.

'What does he say and how do you know – does he telephone you?' Judy asked gently. Thelma often said that half Sheila's unhappiness lay in the fact that people weren't interested in her. She was a clown and her family had made her bitterly conscious of it.

Sheila brightened at Judy's question. 'Well, not as often as we'd like but I've been over there once or twice a week since and – well, you know how I feel about the open air and the land and all that. Gosh, I wish I had more time to spend there. You should just hear Victor on the subject of chemical manures and silage. It's poetry!'

'And what did he think about my cousin and this man who is losing his hearing?' Judy gently brought her back to the subject.

'Oh, he said when he was learning to shoot (his uncle likes them all to be nifty with guns) he met a chap there who was losing his hearing and it was awful. They kept shooting close to him to see if he could hear the shot.'

'How awful! You're making it up!' Judy protested.

'Well, it must be partly true, because old Dr Knox (so Katie was telling me) made your cousin Linda sing right up close to Felix Morford–'

'He did *what?* She never told me!' Judy said, without thinking. Then she wished she hadn't, because Sheila looked guilty as if she shouldn't have mentioned it.

'It was a medical experiment,' she said unhappily. 'Easier to turn off than the radio,

I expect.'

'Well, whatever happened?' Judy asked her, really interested.

'I say, I ought not to have mentioned it, because the other fellows wanted her to sing and they got the Sister's permission and she wasn't going to. Well, you know how she's refused to do it for us and the concert and all that. Well, this Felix Morford must have heard a bit of what was going on, or guessed. Anyway, he wrote down a message, asking her to sing, so she did. She was no end popular. Fancy her not telling you! Well, she wouldn't, I suppose – sort of stealing your thunder, the way you played the piano for the chaps!' Sheila said, happily.

Judy was very angry. 'No such thing, Sheila! It was very kind of Linda to sing for them, and just the sort of thing I would have expected her to do. You don't like Linda! Why?'

Thelma came in at that moment and heard it. She and Sheila exchanged unhappy glances. Judy was so devoted to Linda; how could they tell her how they saw her cousin? Thelma said shortly, 'There's someone on the telephone for you, Sheila,' and when Sheila had gone rushing out, sure it would be Victor, she said to Judy, 'I would have told you, but Linda didn't want anyone to know. Not about the singing, I mean, but about this chap Morford. Can't think why.

He hasn't got any money, he's not young and glamorous like your Richard – I suppose she's just awkward about it. As to whether we like her or not, we're not related to her and we haven't known her all the years you have. Have a heart, Judy! She treats us pretty roughly at times.'

Thelma felt like adding that they considered Linda treated Judy no better, but there was no point in upsetting Judy.

So Thelma said, 'There's a story going the rounds that Philip Addison is dating you. You don't have to say anything but you know what the grapevine's like. Everything pointed to you and Rick Cartwright, and now this has cropped up.'

Judy didn't seem to be listening. She said under her breath. 'Poor man!' and looked unseeingly at Philip Addison's big figure striding across the yard below.

'Why? What's he doing?' Thelma jumped up to look.

'Oh, I meant this Felix Morford. Losing his hearing, if he loves opera like that, must be awful. Like … like if I couldn't play the piano any more,' she half whispered.

'Well, that's life,' Thelma said bracingly. 'Funny thing, if you're going to lose the use of something it usually happens to be connected with the thing you like doing best. Isn't that queer?' And as Judy still stared unseeingly into the middle distance, she said, in a very doubtful voice, 'I say, do stop me if I'm trespassing, which I expect I am, but *is* it true about you and Rick or about you and Philip Addison? I mean, it would make life simpler if we could know, your friends, I mean. That is, we could head Linda off, if she was trying to crash in.'

Judy looked at her as if she'd never seen her before. 'I don't know what you're talking about, Thelma. I'm not engaged to anyone and Linda doesn't crash in. She's different to me. We've always gone about together. She just can't get used to splitting up. She hated it when we couldn't work on the same ward.'

Thelma gave it up. It was no use trying to work up to warn Judy that her cousin was no friend to her, or trying to hint to Judy that Linda was saying things, or spreading the impression about certain things, behind her back. Linda's habit was to do it when only one person was there, so that there weren't any witnesses, and her method was devastating – you couldn't pin her down to actual things said. Thelma gave it up.

Linda strolled in when they came off duty and watched Judy changing. 'What's that – a new outfit?' she asked softly.

'No, of course not,' Judy said in surprise. 'That old navy sweater you got tired of, and this skirt belongs to the suit you didn't like. I told you they'd mix and match but you'd never try so stop looking so outraged.'

Linda said, 'Well, is it a secret what you're changing for?'

'No. I'm going to Skidgate Academy of Music,' Judy said unwillingly. She didn't know why she was unwilling to disclose her destination to Linda, but suddenly her cousin was a stranger.

Linda smiled. 'Oh, what a lovely idea! I'll come with you.'

'Actually I'm going with someone,' Judy said.

'Then we'll be three, won't we?' Linda smiled, and nobody had a thicker skin than Linda, when she wanted to push in.

Philip Addison was even less pleased than Judy, to see Linda come out with her. 'Oh, had you forgotten where we were going, Judy?' he asked.

'No. My cousin just walked out of the hospital with me,' Judy said, preparing to get into his car.

'That's right,' Linda agreed. 'Oh, there *is* one thing. I do need to get into Skidgate rather urgently. Would I be an awful bore if I asked for a teensy lift? Drop me at the Bull Ring and I promise you won't see me again.'

Philip Addison looked helplessly at Judy. He didn't want Linda with them. He had something to ask Judy that was rather important. Judy said, 'You don't mind giving my cousin a lift, do you, Philip?' So he could do little else but agree, knowing full well that as Judy had used his Christian name, Linda would as well, and she did.

'Judy, you have got on well with making friends since you came to this hospital, you know!' she remarked chattily, as they left the town and took the coast road.

'What do you mean?' Judy asked. Every time Philip had started to say something to her, winding through Pollingden's narrow and cluttered streets, Linda had nipped in quickly and stopped him. Now she had settled down to a conversational line of her own.

'Oh, I was thinking of Rick Cartwright, of course. Such a little while it took you to sew that up. Why aren't we bringing him too? Or have you had a row with him?'

Philip waited to hear what Judy would say to that. She was fuming, he could see.

Linda didn't give her much chance. 'Oh, I've put my big foot in it! I'm so sorry! I forgot all about your engagement to him being a secret! Does it matter?'

Philip twitched the wheel ever so slightly, but that was the only sign he gave that he was at all put out. Judy turned round and said furiously, 'I am not engaged to him, and what are you cooking up, Linda, saying that I am?' she burst out.

'Oh, did I misunderstand him? Well, I'm sorry, but there must be something in it, so it can't be just nothing, can it?' and she sat back and left it to Philip and Judy. She had done her little bit of mischief for the time being.

They sat in frosty silence. Judy's throat constricted. It was to have been a lovely afternoon with Philip and his brother at the Music School. Now she could feel the waves of his anger reaching out to touch her almost. Well, what was the matter with him, she asked herself angrily? What sort of friend was he if he had to get so angry just because Linda had broken into their afternoon and hinted things about Rick? Philip knew what Rick was like: goodness, he had warned her. No, he wanted to say I-told-you-so, she said furiously to herself. What else can anyone expect of a flirt like Rick, but rumours and unpleasantness? That's what he wanted to say.

Philip, in the end, said nothing. He felt he had no right to. It was painfully obvious, how much Judy was in love with Cartwright, and Philip was consoling himself with this bit of friendship through music. He knew Cartwright would never marry, and all he asked was to be there to pick up the pieces, when Judy needed him – as she would, Philip was sure.

They arrived at the ornate white building that had once been a Victorian mansion, and Linda expressed pleasure. 'Oh, it looks such a nice place to study at! I'm so glad I made up my mind to it,' and she got out and waited while Judy extricated herself from the front seat.

'What did you say?' Judy asked, coming round to her.

'Surprise, surprise,' Linda said, smiling broadly. 'I'm going to sing for them, and ask them if they'll take me for a pupil. Well, of course, you always said I ought to study singing to the exclusion of everything else, only there, that's me – I just couldn't bear the thought of breaking up our close friendship. And now I need not, because here's a music school on the doorstep,' Linda finished happily.

'But you never mentioned such an idea before,' Judy gasped.

'Well, let's go inside, shall we?' Philip put in. 'Perhaps your cousin doesn't know that the music school is run by my brother. If she wants to study so badly, I dare say I could–'

'Actually it's half-way arranged,' Linda put in, looking down, as she walked. 'You see, it was to please a patient. He knows the head of the music school and suggested it. Felix Morford, you know. Well, what could I lose? He's very happy to have been able to arrange something for me.'

Felix Morford. Philip knew the connection, Judy could see. She sighed. She didn't mind Linda having a musical career nor having a friend in a patient, but it was hard luck that Linda had to come this day, which was to have meant so much to her friendship with Philip.

It was Linda's afternoon, of course. Harold was very thrilled with her voice, and very thrilled to think she was Judy's cousin. 'What a talented family,' he kept saying, and they met the singing master. But from then on, it was a matter of sitting quietly, not even by Philip's side, while Linda held the stage, and sang more than Judy had known her cousin to sing before. Everyone was excited about the beautiful voice, and applauded her, and Linda was scintillating, and kept taking Judy's arm and saying things like, 'My cousin Judy always said–', so that Judy was thoroughly uneasy by the time tea-time came, and they were invited to tea with Harold, in his pleasant study overlooking a tree-lined garden at the back. And then Linda said artlessly, 'It really *was* a pity that Rick couldn't come along. Of course, I know he's much better with fast cars and boats than music but I'm sure he would have been glad for me. He said several times that one of us ought to get moving with music, and I don't suppose you'll bother with that, or with anything, now, Judy–' and she broke off and clapped her hand to her mouth again. 'Oh, I keep forgetting I'm not supposed to mention about you and Rick. He'll be so cross.'

She watched the effect of her words, and saw slow anger in Philip's face, and a sharp interrogating glance in Harold's eyes. So Harold thought his brother was doing nicely with Judy, did he? Linda felt that she had made her contribution to the afternoon and could now sit back and eat the sticky cakes she loved. She had no need to fear putting on the inches; that was Judy's worry, not hers, so she ate happily, and enjoyed Philip's efforts to turn the conversation to Judy's piano playing, which didn't get them far, because obviously there had been some idea of taking it up, but now, until the position was clarified about Judy and Rick Cartwright, nothing apparently could be done.

Judy felt one of those moods coming over her when she could cheerfully have shaken her cousin. It wasn't that she minded about Linda's holding the stage or getting what she wanted by way of music training; it was the way Linda did it. Time and time again in the past, they had had fierce arguments over just such a situation, and Judy remembered, too, the natural outcome of such scenes – Linda would capitulate, say she had been a pig, express sorrow for her way of going on, and promise the earth by way of recompense for Judy, knowing all the time that it was too late. The damage would have been done.

And every time Judy had to step so carefully because of the invidious position Linda always placed her in. As now: it would be so easy, whatever Judy did, to start people accusing her of being jealous of Linda, because after all, as their old music teacher had often said, if a person had a little talent and a lot of determination, she could become a good pianist, but a singer – ah, that was different. A golden voice was a gift from heaven, a thing so personal that you either had it or you didn't. Linda had it.

Judy mentally shrugged off her irritation, but she did say when they got back to the Nurses' Home, 'Linda, you go in. I want to speak to Mr Addison for a moment.'

Linda said easily, 'All right, but don't be a goop and call him that! His name's Philip – try it. He won't mind! I call him that!' and she didn't even notice the way Philip was looking, as if he was hating all of it.

It wasn't the time or the place for a few words to him. Judy could see that. But she did her best. 'I'm so sorry! I didn't know she was coming or that she was going to push in like that or even that the singing lessons had been arranged!'

Philip said tautly, 'Why on earth are you apologising? It seems to have been arranged with my brother. It's nothing to do with me. I was just asked to give a lift. I'd do that for anyone.'

Judy bit her lip. 'Yes, well, apart from that, don't take any notice of what Linda said about Rick and me. It isn't true. He did say he cared for me but he also said he wasn't a marrying man and anyway, I wouldn't want to marry him, not now.' But again Philip wouldn't let her continue.

'That, too, is nothing to do with me,' he said quietly.

'But I thought we were to be friends, you and I,' Judy said desperately.

He looked at her and his eyes were chilly. 'I don't feel that Cartwright would care for his fiancée to insist on a friendship with one of the consultants, do you?' and Judy could see that in his present mood he was more prepared to believe Linda than herself, and that she was in fact engaged to Rick Cartwright.

It was that innocent air of having blurted something out, Judy thought, as she hurried up the stairs, her throat tight with emotion, at the thought of the way this afternoon had turned out for her. If Linda had said outright that she was engaged to Rick, it might have sounded wrong, but no – Linda had cleverly managed to look thoroughly dismayed at having let slip such a piece of information.

The old aunt had always said that Judy had the temperament of a redhead, not Linda. Judy's anger welled up when she found Linda the centre of an admiring circle in their shared bedroom. 'Oh, and you simply mustn't let anyone know I told you!' she was saying, and almost managed to look as if she were on the point of blushing when Judy came into the room. 'Well, Philip Addison and his brother know, so it isn't a secret any longer, is it?' she said quickly before Judy could speak.

Judy said thickly, forcing the words out, 'Everyone, listen to me, because I'm the person in the position to know. I simply am not engaged to Rick Cartwright – there's no talk of an engagement. And all of you must know very well that he isn't the marrying type, anyway!'

There was a sort of blank silence that happens when the wrong thing has been said. The other young nurses looked at each other, and at Linda, whose face was smooth and undismayed as she said quietly, 'I thought you wanted to keep that to yourself? I wasn't talking about that at all! What I was telling them was the gorgeous story of my voice being trained by Philip Addison's brother's music school!'

Chapter Eight

The days that followed were lonely ones for Judy. Rick, who had heard of what happened in their bedroom, seemed to be keeping out of her way. Philip Addison, who had *not* heard what had happened in their shared room that day, also kept out of the way, nurturing the conviction that Judy and Rick were keeping their engagement a splendid secret, as nothing was being said about it and the grapevine had never been so quiet. As for Linda, something quite different kept her out of Judy's way.

In the Men's Ward where Felix Morford was, was also a patient called Maurice Timbrell. He had come into the Accident wing with broken ribs and cuts and abrasions after a car accident, and then been removed to Joseph Ward on discovery of an ulcer. 'You know of course what he is?' Thelma asked Judy.

'Now how should I know?' Judy smiled. 'I only went on that ward to play the piano to that poor boy, and he died before I could go again.' And the smile vanished rather too quickly.

'I know, and for goodness' sake don't let

Home Sister know you feel so badly about it. Well, goodness, you look as if you're about to bawl, whatever you may say by way of denying it! No, I meant, Maurice Timbrell is in show bizz, and your cousin Linda's making up to him with a view to leaving the nursing profession and getting a singing part.'

'Thelma, you girls! The things you come out with!' Judy exploded. 'Linda's only going to be trained at the Skidgate School of Music because she likes singing–'

'Is that why she's got special permission to sing to Felix Morford every afternoon, to see if he can hear the teeniest sound?' Thelma asked, smiling wryly. 'There are certain people who are cattily saying that it's as good a way of getting an audition as any! But there, I don't suppose you'll believe it unless Linda tells you, and she won't.'

'Why are you so sure that she won't tell me when she's ready?'

'Oh, don't keep taking up the cudgels on her behalf, Judy – you don't have to. You're big girls now! She's doing it because she is determined to have as many irons in the fire as she can and because she can't find a suitable rich doctor to marry her. I am quoting her,' she finished fiercely, as Judy turned on her.

Judy calmed down. 'She doesn't want Richard Cartwright, and I'm sure he'd forget he wasn't the marrying type if she did.'

'Don't you believe it. That chappie's keen on you and doesn't really know what hit him, so he's keeping out of your way, hoping the feeling will go off, in case he absent-mindedly proposes to you one day when he's not really as wide awake as he should be!'

'I wish you wouldn't go on like this, Thelma,' Judy fretted. 'You seem such a nice sensible girl until you start thinking about Linda, and then you go all odd and say uncharitable things and it isn't like you.'

On the day that Felix Morford had his next operation, Linda made it her business to find Judy to ask her a favour. Judy had already heard the others talking about Felix. From their conversation she learned that he was in his early thirties, and had had a thriving business of his own before his accident in his own car, swerving to miss a child who had run out into the road. His operations were for legs and back. His ear operation was being put off until the last. It was unlikely that he would be out of hospital for many months.

Linda caught Judy at the second landing. Judy had stopped to look out at Philip Addison striding towards the car park, and had paused to wonder why she missed his friendship more than the one-sided pleasure that had been all she had got out of her meetings with Rick Cartwright.

Linda said urgently, 'Judy, do something for me, will you? It's very, very important!'

'If I can,' Judy said readily. 'What is it?'

'Well, I hardly know how to ask you,' Linda said, with rare hesitation, and she glanced at what could be seen of Judy's now close-cut brown hair under her cap.

'Well, don't take too long because I've got a message for Sister Curzon and you know what she's like,' Judy smiled.

'Well, you know that red wig I've got? Would you wear it? Just to walk down to the gate in, I mean. With your coat on, as if you were going out,' Linda finished, all in a rush.

'Now just a minute! What are you cooking up now?' Judy said.

'Look, I want someone to think I'm going out this afternoon – someone in our ward. They will be watching from the window.'

'Who will be? What's it all about?' Judy insisted.

'Oh, it doesn't matter who! Well, all right then, you won't know him, but it's a chap called Inns. There was a time when you would do anything for me without questioning me!'

'Not this time. It sounds hole and corner. If you can't tell me straight out what it's all about, I won't help.'

'All right,' Linda sighed wearily. 'Inns will

be watching and will tell Felix Morford when he comes down from theatre. Felix made me promise to go out this afternoon for a walk and get some air.'

'Well, why don't you go, and wave up to the window so that Inns can see it's really you?' Judy asked reasonably.

'Because I've got something else to do!' Linda retorted.

Judy thought about it. 'I see. With someone else. Someone you haven't mentioned to Felix Morford, is that it? He cares for you, doesn't he? Why can't you do just one thing the poor chap wants, without being devious and trying to make me do something shabby?'

'It isn't any use lecturing me or trying to make me feel small. If you won't do it, I'll ask Sheila to wear the wig but it won't do, because she can't walk like me, and it'll all be spoilt. It's such a small thing to ask. Well, if you won't wear the red wig, will you wear that hideous scarf of mine that you don't like – how about that?'

'Who are you going out with?' Judy asked quietly.

Linda thought quickly. 'Look, the thing is, what I'm doing is a surprise for Felix. Rick has offered to drive me into Skidgate to a shop there, to get a present for Felix – something I can't get in Pollingden. It's a little book he's been wanting, if you must know.

135

And if I could have persuaded anyone else to drive me there quickly instead of that futile boy, Rick, I would, believe me. *Now* will you do it?'

'Well, that's different! I think that's very nice of you, Linda, to want to give poor Felix Morford a little gift. Of course I'll do it, though I wish it didn't have to be something like pretending to be you. You know I don't like that.'

'Will you do it?' Linda urged. 'That poor Felix Morford has got three more operations coming up and he only knows about one.'

Judy capitulated. They said Linda hadn't a heart, but didn't this prove how wrong they all were? 'Let's make it good, with the old red wig, then,' she said wildly, laughing with Linda.

Philip was doing the operation. Inns, at the window, said under his breath to his neighbour 'She's just going out now. So it was all lies about her. You never can tell, can you?'

His neighbour could get up to go out to the bathroom, so he scrambled out of bed to look out of the window. They watched the girl with the red hair, and decided that that was Linda's walk, Linda's way of holding her head, Linda's off-duty clothes. And for good measure, Judy, in the red wig, turned round and raised a hand to them. That settled them. Inns said, 'Well! I take back all I said about that girl. Poor old Morford, who'd have thought it, then?'

Maurice Timbrell looked surprised. 'Are you sure it's Linda?'

'Have a look, mate,' Inns said, putting up his thumb, in a gesture of approval about Linda. 'I know you can't get up but you can use that hand mirror of yours, can't you?'

Maurice Timbrell got his mirror and held it up just in time to see Judy going out of the hospital gate. 'That's funny,' he said. He called a young nurse who was going past the end of his bed. 'Tell me where Linda goes – which direction,' he asked her.

The nurses all did things for Maurice. The magic aura of his profession gave him a glamour he hardly realised. The nurse said, 'Linda Lawrence? Don't be silly!' and laughed, but he kept pointing, so she stood on tiptoe and looked, and murmured to herself, 'That's funny.'

'There are two of them, aren't there?' he murmured, so that Inns shouldn't hear. Inns was arguing noisily with someone two beds further down, about the date that Felix Morford had entered hospital. 'And that one isn't Linda!'

'But it must be!' the girl said, puzzled. 'Judy, the other one, has had her hair dyed back to brown, and cut very short. Besides, Judy doesn't–' She had been going to say that Judy didn't walk like that, anyway, until she remembered things she had heard about them. 'What does it matter, anyway?' she laughed.

'Well, it does, you see. Poor old Morford is silly over Linda and thinks she's going to stay in this afternoon crying over his operation in case it doesn't turn out right. He made her promise to go out for a walk.' He nodded to the girl, but she wasn't going to get involved, and said, 'Well, she's done what he wanted – good for her!' and hurriedly left him.

Maurice was intrigued. A lifetime in show business gave him an instinct for good acting, and that was good. He couldn't have said how – it looked like Linda all over, but he felt it was out of character for her to do what Morford wanted. Linda was a go-go type and hard-boiled as they came. He was used to that and understood it. He would have been surprised if a girl with a voice like that hadn't been determined to let him hear it, though for him a voice was no good without the acting ability and everything else with it. She had the tricks, but no warmth and she didn't understand that warmth was necessary. And he couldn't stomach the way she had got permission to sing, leading the ward sister and poor Morford to think it was for him, not for a free audition. But this other girl, the one who had been playing the piano the day that he had been brought up here?

He had been feeling so ill that day, he had wished that piano to be miles away, but she had played soft soothing music for the chap who had died, and she had come round the ward and said a few words to everyone. He himself had shut his eyes and not encouraged jolly chat with a strange nurse, but he now remembered that she had said, in a warm friendly voice, 'Feeling rotten? All right, I won't bother you,' and had gone quietly to the next bed. Yes, now he remembered her! He had her pinpointed in his mind, very dark eyes as well. Deep dark eyes, where the smile began. Now, if that girl was the one doing Linda's walk, then she might just be what he was looking for, but instinct told him she wouldn't be interested. Later that afternoon, he heard, by careful questioning of another nurse, the way Judy was treated by Linda, and the way Linda had broken up that friendship with Dr Cartwright. The nurse also admitted that Judy was no longer going around with Philip Addison, which, Maurice Timbrell thought, was a pity. They would make a couple of nice people, those two.

Linda's and Judy's times were different now they had been split up. Linda had the rest of the day off but Judy had only two hours, and as she walked towards the Post Office, cutting through the narrow passage between the old church and the antique shop, she saw Rick Cartwright looking in the side window, at the display of card tables. He looked up and saw her, his jaw dropping.

She was no less staggered. 'Where's Linda?' she gasped.

'What is more to the point,' he gritted, 'What on earth do you think you're doing?' and his eyes went up to the red wig.

She tore it off. 'Oh, this was what she asked me to do. Never mind that – did she find the book in the shop in Skidgate?'

'How should I know? I haven't seen her for two days!'

'Now listen,' Judy said desperately, 'who's playing the joke on me – you or Linda?' and she told him briefly what Linda had asked her to do.

He was frankly scornful. 'And you fell for that? You little idiot! She was having you on! I don't know who she's with or why this story's cooked up, but you can believe this – I wouldn't give your cousin Linda a lift in my car if it was the only transport within miles! And you know why!'

'I don't,' Judy said, white to the lips.

He took her arms. 'Judy, don't be an idiot. I love you. I would even ask you again to marry me. But I couldn't, wouldn't settle for a life ahead for myself in which that girl was. She's ... she's–'

'Don't say it! Don't say anything about Linda!' Judy gasped. 'You don't like her, you never have, but you can't expect me to be pleased to hear it!'

Rick drew a deep breath, and said, 'Look, there's a tea-shop down here. I think you could do with a cup. I know I could! And at least we can talk!'

'I don't want to talk to you, Rick!'

'Well, I want to talk to you, Judy, about a lot of things.'

It was a tea-shop that opened on to the main road as well as to this quiet passage. Rick found a table in the window looking over the churchyard. The soft green of the overhanging trees and the old knobbly grey stones of the church and wall were soothing to the eye, and they sat sipping hot sweet tea and ignoring the biscuits, while they framed what they should say, both speaking at once and halting, just like strangers. Well, we are strangers now, Judy thought miserably.

Rick was thinking it too. 'Judy, is it true you didn't want to see me? That's what Linda told me. She said you didn't want me bothering you because I hadn't marriage to offer. Is that true?'

It was true that that was what Judy had secretly wanted, but a flame of anger shot through her that Linda should have taken it on herself to tell Rick so, and that Linda should have read Judy's thoughts so correctly. She said, 'Let's not discuss whether it's true or not. Whatever I say about my cousin Linda's intentions, you won't believe it. Answer me this, Rick: why did you ever start showing me any liking at all? I mean, I must have made it obvious from the start that I wasn't the sort to – well, just flirt around – they say a man can tell, just by the first look. Isn't it true?'

He laughed shortly, ruefully. 'In the main, yes, unless he's a bighead, which you might say I am. I suppose I receive that sort of thing from girls, all girls, and it never occurred to me that there would be just one who'd invite me to go jump in the sea. Well, you looked as if you were thinking that, even if you didn't say it!'

'Oh, Rick, I never did!' she protested.

'Judy, I don't want to lose you, love. Tell me honestly, is there anyone else? What about Addison? I've seen you around with him! Well, if it's that way with him, then say so. At least give me the truth, so I don't have to be worried by what Linda tells me. Yes, well, it's no use looking like that, because Linda we have with us all the time and what Linda does with that clever tongue of hers is– Oh, Judy, all right, I'm sorry, I take it all back. Honestly! Just tell me, is it Philip Addison you're keen on? You've only got to say!'

'If you must know, there's only one person I'm keen on and it won't do me any good, because if you can't believe what I say then what's the use of anything?' she stormed.

He put out a hand and enclosed hers in it.

He had never held her hand like this. He turned it over, looking at it as if he had never seen it before. 'Sometimes I think I am going to capitulate and marry you, in spite of everything,' he murmured. 'It's what you do to me. It isn't comfortable and I can't even say I like it. But it's there, nagging all the time.'

She was shocked. 'What is, Rick? Tell me what effect I have on you?' she said, leaning forward.

He shrugged, but still held her hand. 'I'm not much good at words. I just feel wretched most of the time. I feel as if I've lost something, and I don't like that! I've always been able to get what I wanted, when I wanted it. Now it's different.'

'That's bad, Rick,' she said, thinking of the aching longing, the lost horrible lonely feeling she felt herself.

'Couldn't we make a go of it, Judy? You and me?' he asked suddenly. 'I'm not proposing, so don't throw anything at me! I'm just talking aloud. See, we like boating and swimming–'

'But that isn't enough to build a marriage on,' she said.

'And we're in love,' he added.

'But it wouldn't be enough for you. You'd want other girls.'

'You'd have everything you wanted, money-wise–'

She shook her head. 'You're just being a little child, Rick, crying for the moon. So am I. It won't work. I know it. Let's both get used to doing without being in love with each other.'

Suddenly he lifted her hand to his lips. He didn't know why he did it. Just the touch of her hand against his lips, comforted him in some queer way, but it was so unlike him, and it was just stirring the agony. Two tears welled over the lids of Judy's eyes and for a moment the world was blotted out. She didn't see Philip Addison, on his way to the Post Office, stop for a startled moment, look at them both, and walk on, his eyes on the ground. Neither did Rick. He was battling with the thought that he must, for the first time in his life, say no to something he wanted, because he knew that if he did marry Judy, she would change things, keep him from flirting with other girls, for a start. Most of all she would give him a strong feeling of responsibility, being tied down, which horrified him.

'Let's go,' she said, blinking fiercely. 'I've had enough. Besides, I have to be back and I want to know where Linda is.'

'How that girl creeps in!' he jeered softly. 'She's of age. Let her be, Judy, for goodness sake.'

'You don't understand!' she said, forgetting her covering up for Linda, because she was so cross with Rick's constant harping. 'I wore this wig so that Linda could go and buy a surprise present for Felix Morford,' and she explained just what had been involved. 'So if you didn't drive her to Skidgate, then who did?'

He stared. 'Judy, you don't mean to tell me you believed that stuff, surely? Any fool would know that wasn't in character! Well, honestly, Linda doesn't *do* those things!'

Judy was so furious, she turned and left him. He watched her go into the Ladies' Room, and while he was settling the bill for the tea, she came out with the wig on again. She was, he had to concede, very good at pretending to be Linda – as good as Linda was at pretending to be Judy. He wondered uneasily just what Linda was up to.

Oddly it was Philip Addison who settled that. Having seen Judy herself, sitting at the table in that tea-shop with Rick kissing her hand, he was very much surprised to see her walking back with the wig on. In fact, the walk fooled him at first. 'Linda?' he said sharply, but when she turned, he saw it was Judy.

'Well, I thought I was taking leave of my senses for a moment,' he said, 'because she couldn't have got back in time.'

'Back from where?' Judy demanded.

'You mean you didn't know? Then what are you doing with that wig on?' so Judy told him what the plan had been. 'Oh, I should have told Rick not to let poor Felix Morford know!'

'I doubt it will matter,' Philip said dryly. 'She wanted to meet the impresario who was visiting my brother's school of music. Why are you looking so astonished?'

'But why couldn't she tell me. Why make up this story and persuade me to act the fool with this wig on, and deceive those nice men on Joseph Ward? Why, why?' She looked crushed. He couldn't take his eyes off her. He wanted to gather her to him and tell her to stop carrying the torch for Linda, but he had seen her with Rick, in that very intimate little tableau in the tea-shop. 'Why didn't you ask Cartwright?' he asked harshly.

'Because, if you want to know, everyone is only too willing to make me think my cousin Linda is everything that is rotten.'

'Well,' he asked.

'Well, she may be selfish and out for her own ends, but how many of us can say we aren't like that too?' Judy stormed.

'I suppose,' he said, studying his pipe and finally getting out tobacco and starting to repack it, 'she is one of those people who must be devious. Perhaps it seemed logical to her to play-act in this way, rather than to take the dull way out of just telling you what she wanted to do.' It was his effort to be kind, let her down lightly, because he could

146

suddenly see just how much Linda meant to her, and why. But Judy didn't see it like that. She thought it was his way of being cleverly critical.

'Well, all I hope is that one day, *some* day, someone will see some good in my cousin Linda, because it's very boring as it is, to be eternally told bad things about her which I know are just not true.'

The things that happened in those two hours off duty had made Judy tired. A sort of mental exhaustion set in, but she remembered to walk in the gates like Linda, for the benefit of the watching men. She went back on duty, ready to do battle with anyone if they so much as mentioned her cousin. But nobody did, as Linda had the rest of the day off, and there were two emergencies. Judy, loving her work in hospital, saw each emergency, each new admission, as something interesting opening up before her eyes. No two cases were ever alike. She had her tea, and her evening meal, and only when it was dark, and the others came bouncing back from a lecture, did Judy start worrying about Linda.

It was not Rick – who was, after all, on the medical side and should have been the one – who told her. It was Philip Addison who sent for her, and told her, as gently as he could, that her cousin had collapsed in Skidgate High Street, and had been taken to the hospital there, until it was discovered she was on the staff of St Paul's Hospital in Pollingden.

'Collapsed? But I don't understand. She's as fit as fiddle – you don't mean she was run over?' Judy cried.

Phillip looked over her head. 'Judy, she's picked up a bug.'

'A what? *Linda?*' Judy couldn't believe it. In their young days it was herself who had got the illnesses, Linda, the frail-looking child of the two had been wiry and strong.

'She's been admitted to the Isolation Wing,' he said quietly.

Chapter Nine

The cousins had become more a subject of interest in the hospital than either of them had realised. It spread like wildfire, the news that Linda Lawrence was in Isolation but just what sort of bug she had picked up, hadn't been released.

Rick's chief – Dr Foy – was in charge of the case and questioned Judy closely, which puzzled her a great deal.

'I want you to tell me exactly who your cousin went out with, for the purposes of tracing the bug,' he said gently. 'It is a little-known one but we do know it and we do know where it comes from. Now, has she been friends with anyone from the Middle East? Think carefully.'

Judy looked stupefied. 'Oh, no, sir. We usually go out together, or at least, which-ever friend I have, my cousin takes her turn with next time,' and she blushed at the way he looked at her. 'I must explain – we are very close. We've been brought up together. We always have done that. Shared our friends, I mean.'

'Well, when she is not going out with your friend, who is she with, and who is she with when *you* are not with her, as I know for a fact that your times have been changed with your duty.'

Judy blinked. She had forgotten that factor for the moment, it had been such a shock to find her cousin whisked away to a part of the hospital that she had no entry into. 'I can't think. I suppose she would tell me if she'd met someone else – like, for instance, the impresario she had been going to the Music School to see.'

'Then I want you to do some detective work and find out just who your cousin has been seeing, because that person may be a carrier and start an epidemic, and no hospital in the area could hope to cope. You understand, don't you?'

St Paul's was too old and ill-fitted for an epidemic, she thought dully. But what about the brassy new hospital in Skidgate? He read her thoughts, it seemed. 'Skidgate's modern aspect is all for casualty, not for research – even poor old St Paul's is better equipped in that aspect,' he said dryly.

Judy's eyes blindly met his. Why was Rick's boss talking to her like this? She who was only a little First Year? She decided that Linda was going to die, and it was insupportable.

She must have cried out the thought. He held her shoulder in a brief hard clasp. 'No, my dear, that was not my intention – I don't even know what her chances are yet. We haven't enough information. But she is pinning her faith on you, so you must play your part and believe she'll be all right. You do understand?'

'You mean I can see her, sir?'

It appeared she would be allowed in, suitably gowned and wearing a mask, for just a little while.

It was an unreal and alarming conversation. She stumbled down to her section again. She met Rick on the way. He clasped her by the shoulders, and said, 'Judy, I'm sorry, I didn't know!'

'What do you mean, Rick?'

'Well, you've been told what's the matter with her, I presume?' he said in surprise. Nobody had told him not to tell Judy.

She thought he was referring to the conversation she had just had, and nodded. 'I've got to do some detective work and find out who she knew who could have come from the Middle East,' she said, still in that stupefied voice.

Rick slowly flushed because she was looking so hard at him. Should he tell her what he knew of Linda's circle of friends outside the hospital? He decided against it. Since he had seen Judy last, he had been thinking, and finally revolted against involvement. Judy was drugging him with her love for him, and he was slowly sinking into a mire of deeper feeling for her than he had ever intended to feel toward any girl. Get out – his thoughts jangled – while there's time!

'Will you help me, Rick?' she whispered.

'Sure, love,' he told her. 'Any time. Just find me and tell me what you want, and old Rick will be there. And don't worry!' he patted her shoulder, and left her standing there, and if he'd said an outright No, shouted from the rooftops, he couldn't have made it more plain.

The empty feeling intensified. She went down to the basement with the note with details for a file Sister Curzon wanted, and while she waited, she remembered that Linda had been on unspecified trips at least five times, giving Judy the impression that she had been out with Rick. Either Rick had lied or Linda had used him to cover for somebody else. Judy decided Rick wasn't lying. He had been out with Linda two or three times but lost interest. That was Rick: never pursue someone who bored him. Never pursue someone who was too obvious, either. But could Linda have been accused of being boring or too obvious? Judy's loyalty was stretched, and she abandoned the thought, and remembered another washer that one of the taps needed. The boilerman!

He was an extremely skinny, gloomy looking man, from the back streets of Pollingden.

He looked at her hair. He remembered she had been red not so long ago. 'I like 'em red,' he remarked. 'Like your cousin. Sorry about her, nurse. So's our Pete. Said to tell you, special.'

'Who is your Pete?' Judy asked, in alarm.

The boilerman searched for a washer, and muttered, 'My young brother. Took her on the back of his bike, he did, when she couldn't get somewhere in a hurry. She never sniffed at any transport. Anything for a laugh, that girl.'

It was a shock to Judy. At first she didn't believe it until one of the ambulance men confirmed that he had seen Nurse Lawrence on Pete's bike. 'We gave her a lift one day, too. She never minded so long as it was a wheel to get her somewhere,' and he laughed and then sobered and said he was sorry to hear of her illness.

Philip Addison found her in the town's park, near to closing time. He sometimes used it as a short cut. There was no private place to cry at the hospital. Some nurses used the linen room. Judy had been sent out by Home Sister for some air and the pent-up tears of weeks burst their flood-gates on a deserted seat behind a screen of hedge near where the gardeners burnt the refuse. Philip came to this corner of the park on the look-out for a boy whose father had been a patient once. A boy with a lost look in his eyes, because they hadn't been able to save his father. Philip often followed up a case like this. It grieved him so much they had to lose any patient. The boy wasn't there but Judy was, bent double, taut as a spring, her grief breaking her.

He sat down by her, and turned her round. She 'homed' to his shoulder just as the children did, in the hospital. It was some time before she could stop crying.

'Where's Cartwright?' Philip couldn't prevent himself from asking the question. Cartwright shouldn't have let her come out alone. What was the fellow thinking of? He wasn't on duty!

'It doesn't matter where he is,' she choked.

'What does that mean? You two had a row?'

She shook her head. 'No, it's just quietly died, because it should never have started. Do you know, sir, I don't think much of the state of being in love. I'd rather never have experienced it.'

'That's not really true, is it, or else why are you crying?'

'Not for that!' she said quickly. 'I'm just – well, it was the end of everything. My cousin Linda–'

'She'll get better,' he said, as if stating a fact.

She shook her head. 'No, you don't understand. Dr Foy said I was to find out who she'd been with. To stop an epidemic.'

'And you've found out?'

He winced, the way she looked at him. 'I thought we were so close, Linda and I. She's been living a different life, and I never knew!' she choked, as if the words were forced from her.

He didn't comment on that. He had his own views of the tricky Linda. 'But you found out something?'

'I made a start. But I can't do much without transport. I did ask Rick, and he said of course he'd help, but he's so busy.'

'Why didn't you ask me? I'm not busy,' he said grimly. 'When I come off duty I have nothing in the world to do.'

She thought about it, wiped her wet cheek with the back of her hand, and accepted that. 'I learned that the boilerman's young brother gives her lifts on the back of his bike and so do the ambulance men, so where do we go from there?'

'Find out just where they did take her,' Philip Addison said shortly. 'Come on, lass, let's make a start now.'

He had left his car near the park. As they were getting into it, she said, 'Of course, I suppose we should have asked your brother if any of the students have Middle East contacts – well, you said yourself that was where she was going that afternoon.'

He waited until Judy was sitting beside

him and he was smoothly driving out of the car park before he said, 'Why? She never got there. It seems she laid a lot of false trails so we shouldn't know where she did get to – then, and on previous times off.'

'But she always went to the Music School!' Judy protested.

'No. I've already questioned my brother. She went that first day but no more. No, we have to start back at the beginning.'

But it was different now, with Philip Addison to drive her around and do the questioning. He asked if they remembered a redhead, and then Judy put on the wig and walked like her cousin, and in two days they found out what they wanted to know. And a very sick young man was brought into the hospital's Isolation Wing.

'She met him at the photographer's in Skidgate,' Judy said wearily, when Thelma and Sheila questioned her. 'He'd just come back from the Middle East. A young naval officer. Waiting for his photo to be taken for his mother. They went dancing and met whenever she could get out.' Her voice was flat, spent. Linda, who demanded to know every detail of Judy's life, had managed to keep all this from her, and it hurt Judy unbelievably. 'No, he hadn't much money, but people say they were dotty about each other.' She shrugged. 'And now they can get cracking and make her better.'

Make her better. That was dating from their childhood, Judy remembered, as she went to put on the cap, gown and mask, and pay her daily visit to her cousin, who was tearing her hair out in a fever, and calling only for Judy.

'They'll cut all that hair off,' Thelma warned. 'If the fever won't abate with the drugs.' Judy said shortly, 'They have. It looks awful. All curling tight to her head. And she looks–' She couldn't bring herself to say what Linda looked like, with the hectic flush of fever, her eyes wild, and her voice...

That day, in a rare lucid moment, Linda said hoarsely, 'Stay with me, Judy!' The old request. Judy's heart warmed again. Linda did want her! But the urgency was for some other reason, that even pierced the intensity of her fever. Linda continued, 'Don't go out with Rick! He's not for you! Stay here with me!'

Was it possible, ill as she was, to be so possessive? It seemed so. When Judy said, 'Don't worry, Linda, love, that's all over. I'm not seeing Rick any more,' Linda subsided, and dozed fitfully.

That evening Philip said to Judy, 'I wish you didn't have to see your cousin. I don't want you picking up that bug!'

'Oh, what does it matter?' Judy asked wearily. 'How long will it take to reduce the fever?'

He was silent for a while, then said, 'You'll have to know sooner or later, my dear. Reducing the fever isn't the end of it. It's operable, and ... we're going to take a chance, if you agree – will you?'

'Why me?' she asked, and then realised; she was Linda's only next-of-kin. 'Oh, must you operate? The scar!' and oddly she hadn't thought of Linda's voice.

'Plastic surgery works wonders,' Philip soothed, letting it go at that. And when she asked if it would effect a cure, he said. 'The only cure, my dear.'

Every day Judy went to see Felix Morford, who was fretting. He was coming up for his spinal operation any day now, so she made light of her cousin's illness. 'She's young and strong. She won't be long now, before she's about again!' she assured him.

'She sang so beautifully,' he told Judy. 'I did hear it, in the distance. I can't wait for my ear operation!'

Judy smiled, but terror caught her heart. This poor man was apparently in earnest – he was really in love with her cousin. Was he going to be hurt too?

'I'm not hard up, you know,' he told Judy, so she nodded and smiled obligingly, and wrote on the pad for him to read, 'Do you know it isn't permitted for a nurse to be friends with a patient?'

He nodded vigorously. 'Oh, yes, I know,

but I've told Sister and they are making a rather special case of me. You see, I am trying to persuade your cousin to give up nursing and study singing. My interest is opera.'

'Oh, but she isn't good enough for that,' Judy protested, 'I think she knows it, too.'

'It was such a beautiful voice,' he said, remembering. 'She sang very close to my ear. It was so rich and full. Has she – is there anyone, definite, in her life?' he stumbled.

'She isn't engaged to be married,' Judy wrote firmly.

'She told me she loved me,' Felix Morford said, looking at his hands. 'It's the only worthwhile thing I have in life, the only thing that's keeping me going. To get through my operations and to get my hearing back, with your cousin waiting to marry me. She won't be hard up, you know,' he finished earnestly, as if he knew how much money and comfort meant to Linda.

Judy couldn't think of anything to say. She ought to say, My cousin was so much in love with a man, she kept him secret and caught this bug off him and now they are both very ill indeed in this hospital. But how could one say that?

Felix Morford held on to Judy's hand. 'Would *you* object, if … she said yes to me?'

She looked at him. He had such a kind face. In his way he was a little like Philip

159

Addison, she found herself thinking. He would be the sort of man her cousin could lean on, when she was in need of comfort and advice. Linda was about as insecure as anyone Judy had met, and that had always puzzled her. Linda roared through life, charming people, fastening on to this person, claiming the allegiance of that one; taking this girl's man-friend from her, breaking into Judy's arrangements and expecting to be forgiven, because she was Linda Lawrence. And then underneath she would crack and want comforting, reassuring, before she stormed out again. No wonder Rick hadn't wanted to pursue the affair. He was too much like Linda. He, too, wanted someone strong. One day he would marry, she thought, for just that reason. But it would never be someone like Linda. Linda needed a strong man and here was one who wanted her so much.

She smiled brilliantly at Felix Morford and wrote, 'I should like it very much!'

She left the ward with the memory of his quiet happy smile as he lay back with closed eyes.

The next time she saw Linda, she mentioned him to her, but Linda didn't want to hear about him. 'There's a – there's someone – someone called Nigel–' It hurt her throat to talk. She wasn't supposed to, but it was no use trying to stop Linda from doing anything she didn't want to.

Judy sat back with a gasp. The naval officer's name was Nigel – could it be that Linda was going to tell her all about it?

Judy nodded, and said, 'Yes, pet, I know. But don't talk.'

'Want him! Want him!' Like a child, demanding and expecting to get, at the double. 'He knows I'm ill – you've told him? Then why doesn't he come?'

It broke Judy's heart, and she was glad when she was told she couldn't go to see her cousin any more before the operation. That harsh voice, that had taken the place of the golden voice Linda had had, calling for Judy so much that Philip was worried.

He said as she went downstairs, 'I've got permission from Sister to take you out for the evening. I'm going to take you to an old patient's house. It will be quite different from anything you've done–'

'Oh, no, I don't want to meet anyone,' Judy said wildly.

'He's blind,' Philip said. 'We are going to dine with him. And then we'll explore the town. Do you know Oakmere?'

Home Sister did her share of pressure on Judy to get out of the hospital for a few hours, so she put on a quiet golden colour dress and matching coat, trimmed with dark fur, that made her hair look a richer brown, and her eyes a deeper colour. She didn't consciously choose the outfit; it was the best she had, and she was sure that Philip Addison would expect it. He didn't fling money around as Rick was fond of doing, but he always looked well-dressed when he was in mufti, and his car was a quality vehicle, not a flashy roadster like Rick's. With this in mind she took trouble over how she looked. Thelma said approvingly, 'That's right, take a break and forget things. You can help your cousin better that way, you know?'

'How?' Judy choked.

'Because you might ease out tonight. Think she can't sense how taut you are? If she's got any sense, she'll wonder why. You don't want her to think she's more ill than she is, do you?'

Judy said, 'Oh, I see what you mean. Thanks, Thelma.' But it wasn't what Thelma had really meant. She met Sheila's eyes over Judy's bent head, and shook her head at Sheila in case poor Sheila blurted out the truth, in her present silly happy mood over her farmer, who was steadily working up to invite her, Thelma guessed, to leave the nursing scene and marry him. Sheila was a little 'high' these days. It would have been better if Sheila hadn't heard that the naval officer was getting worse and was not likely to survive the operation that Linda was due for the next day.

Judy let herself ease out, once she was in Philip Addison's car. There was nothing more she could do, and she had a sense of being cut off from making effort. They had striven so hard to find the contact, and then … there was no more effort needed. All she could do was to wait.

'When are you operating on my cousin?' she asked suddenly. 'What time tomorrow, I mean?'

'She's second on the list – after the young man,' Philip said, with no great pleasure.

'What sort of operation is it? Would you be prepared to tell me?' and he said, 'No. I never did believe in discussing an operation before it happened, with a relative. Too much emotion to see the thing clearly. You just forget about it, Judy, and have faith.' There was a tiny pause, before he asked, '*Have* you got faith in me, Judy?'

'Yes! Yes, I have! Of course I have!' She was surprised that he should ask such a question.

'It doesn't rest entirely with the surgeon. There are other factors. You know that, of course?'

'If you mean the patient sometimes collapses, I know that, but my cousin Linda is strong. She always has been the strong one though we always thought she was frail.'

He didn't answer that, but began to talk about his friend, the old patient that they were going to see. 'He's blind because the operation that was tried, didn't work. Don't be shy with him – he likes to feel that he's like other people. Don't try to help him – so long as nothing is moved, he can get about and do things for himself. He is proud of his capabilities.'

'Is he an old man?'

'He's my age,' Philip said. 'Do you know how old I am?'

Judy indignantly repudiated having even thought about it.

'That's a pity. Friends should know everything about each other,' he said quietly. 'I am thirty-three.'

'Oh.' Judy didn't know what to say. His age didn't interest her. She saw with surprise that it was what he was, that meant most to her; the kindest man, the rock to lean on when things went wrong, the man who didn't intrude into one's thoughts, but who said and did exactly the right thing at the right time.

'Well?' he asked her with a smile.

'Why didn't you ever marry? You'd have made a wonderful husband,' she said involuntarily.

'There was never time to get round to even thinking about it,' he quietly reminded her. 'I have worked extra hard to get where I am at my age. I dared not waste a minute on anything else.'

'Oh. Yes, of course.' Now the sea was in sight, and down below them, the white spires and grey walls of Oakmere, a town she had wanted to see for so long. But it was Philip who was filling her mind at this moment. 'What sort of person would you have wanted to marry, if you could have taken enough time off to think about it, Philip?' she pursued.

'No sort of person,' he said. 'I would know her when I saw her – the woman I wanted to share my life with. She could be any sort at all. But she'd have to be all heart. That's not a condition, just a necessity for a happy marriage. If a woman hasn't generosity and the capacity for giving, then she isn't going to be able to stand up to the niggling trials of every day that even the most happy marriage is threaded with. I speak from experience – a surgeon gets involved with the lives of his patients whether he wants to or not. I've seen more marriages than you'd believe. We in hospitals see as much of a marriage as the neighbours do – probably a great deal more.' He smiled. 'Aren't I talking a lot tonight?'

'Yes, but I like it. I only asked that question because ... Rick said he would have married me if I hadn't had someone like my cousin Linda in my life. He said he couldn't bear to be married to me and have her there too.'

'Predictable, from that young man,' Philip said quietly. 'You just can't pick and choose, you see. If you know you're looking at *the* one for you, the only one you want for your life partner, then you must take the relatives, the life that's in the past, (because people never relinquish their memories, and their early life has made them what they are!) and the friends they've made and the hobbies they've propped their spare time on. You can't just lift the person out of all that.'

'That's what Rick wanted to do,' she choked.

'And it matters terribly to you, doesn't it, Judy?'

'No. No, I don't think so. I think I'm crying because, well, somehow, one expects so much of the first time one is in love. It really is a shattering business. It fills one's mind, sleeping and waking, but it not only colours everything with excitement, but it also dashes one down. That's what I didn't expect.'

'Perhaps you're going to be one of those fortunate people who will have a very rich and worthwhile second time in love,' he comforted her, as he entered the town, and drove smoothly through the residential part until they reached the high wrought iron gates of a big white Victorian house, where the drive hadn't a weed to be seen, and the lawns were kept so immaculate as to seem artificial. 'Now empty your mind and meet a wonderful person – my ex-patient.'

And after all, it was a wonderful evening. Edward Norris was as tall as Philip but not as strongly built. A graceful man, and Judy felt, the moment she was introduced to him, that he would be a cultured man, with many gifts, many interests to fall back on.

'Tell me what she's like, Philip. Is this the beautiful redhead, or the Murillo brunette?'

Philip said, 'Yes, she has got the look of a Murillo madonna now you come to mention it, Edward. Now how did you sense that?'

Edward Norris's sightless blue eyes stared straight ahead of him but his mouth was puckered with amusement. 'Oh, from the things you carefully said, and those you omitted to say,' he chuckled. 'But my dear,' he said to Judy, 'since I can only imagine what people are like, colours mean little, but the person means a lot. So sit down and tell me about all the things you like to do, while this wicked chap goes and has a look at my man, whose leg he did wonderful things to, not so long ago.'

Edward Norris was easy to talk to, Judy found, and, too, he was not a personal friend, on the spot, with eyes to see, as Philip was, so she could tell him about Linda and her problems.

Philip was gone half an hour, and when he came back, Edward's man came with him, with a trolley on which was the evening meal. Philip saw to the wines, as if he were an old friend in this house, and he talked with the manservant while the round table was being laid. 'I like to do everything in this room,' Edward told Judy. 'I eat here, I listen to my classical music here, I read here, or someone reads from all my books to me,' and he waved a hand to the book-lined walls, whose only break was the place where an extravagant set of hi-fi was housed, together with special deep shelves for his collection of records. 'This is the only room with the sun on it all day. I enjoy it through its warmth on my hands. Play to me, Judy. Philip tells me you do.'

If Philip had intended this evening to be merely a crash venture in taking Judy's mind off Linda, he succeeded more than he knew. It entertained Edward Norris to such an extent that he was inviting Judy to tea on her next free afternoon, which happened to be the following day.

'Oh but I can't! Philip's operating on my cousin Linda,' Judy exclaimed. 'I'm sorry. I should have loved to come.'

'And if you'll take my advice, you *will* come,' Edward said firmly. 'Bad for you, bad for this chap, to have you sitting like an uneasy little ghost outside the operating theatre. No, you come and spend those hours here in this room. Keeping me entertained will take your own mind off things.'

And so it was arranged. But in the event, it never happened. When Judy reached the hospital that night, she found Thelma distracted and Sheila more upset than Judy would have imagined, for so gay a girl.

'What is it?' she asked, her thoughts flying to her cousin.

Thelma shook her head, but Sheila lifted her drowned face and sobbed, 'He's had an accident! He's in our hospital, and he may lose both his legs!' and Thelma said, as if Judy couldn't guess, 'She means Victor Grant.'

Chapter Ten

Both Linda and Judy had already experienced in their short time in the hospital, that special bustle and taut efficiency that heralds an important operation. Today there were three: Linda, the young man she called Nigel, and Sheila's farmer. Dr Foy had never looked so grave, and even Katie Sutcliffe wasn't sharpening the edge of her wit on everything as usual, but went about soberly. This was something new; three operations that had become the private and personal business of two of the nurses.

Sheila was in the Sick Bay, under sedation. Judy said to Thelma, 'I wouldn't have thought she would go to pieces like that!' but Thelma said, 'Wouldn't you? You don't know her family! They take this sort of thing in their stride. They'd probably be just filled with interest. That's what she hates about her home background so much. She's too soft to be a nurse. I wish she'd leave – but there, she'd never have met him if she hadn't stayed here.'

'She really cares for him, doesn't she?' Judy said, looking out of the window. It was their coffee break. It was always too hot and burnt the tongue before one had to dash back to the ward, but today it was a thing they neither of them noticed.

'Yes, she cares,' Thelma said shortly. 'What's going to happen, Judy, if he loses his legs?'

'I don't know. His poor family, too! How did it *happen?*'

'He was riding, and took a hedge that hadn't been clipped, only someone had left a harrow on the other side. They had to kill the horse, too.'

'Oh, no! Oh, I must go to them. Or will you? No, you're Sheila's best friend. You must stay here in case – well, she'd rather have you than me,' Judy said quickly.

'Don't you want to stay and hear about your Linda?'

Judy turned sharply away. 'I wish, in a way, that I could go and see ... the person I met last night. He invited me. I don't want to be here and count the hours. I don't know what I think could go wrong – Philip's operating. He asked me if I had faith in him and I said yes, but had I? Honestly, Thelma, I don't know anything about me any more. I've been too shaken up by everything that's happened in the last few weeks.'

Thelma looked sharply at her. So that was how the land lay! Of course, Philip Addison! Well he would be better for Judy than that tiresome Rick Cartwright. But would Judy ever stop loving Rick? Thelma doubted it. She said, delicately, 'This … person you met last night, how come? I mean, the grapevine had it that Philip Addison had taken you out to a meal. That, moreover, he'd asked special permission of Home Sister to keep you out latish.'

'Oh, the grapevine!' Judy fumed. 'Well, that's true! We went to dine at the house of an old patient of his, a friend, too, I should think. He's a very nice man. Blind.'

Thelma thought about that. She couldn't remember anything having been said about such a patient, but then this was only her First Year, too. Six months longer than Judy, didn't even equip the resourceful Thelma for finding out everything about the surgical top brass. 'Where does he hang out?' she asked.

'Oakmere. Do you know the town?'

'Well, yes, very top drawer. Retired colonels and such. Positively nobody who hasn't had a scintillating career.'

'Oh, Thelma, how you exaggerate!' But it made Judy laugh.

Thelma was encouraged to ask, 'How were you going to get there this afternoon, as Philip Addison isn't at your disposal?'

'Oh, Mr Norris's man was going to fetch me in the Rolls.'

'Was he!' Thelma was impressed, which was saying something. 'And how do you propose to get to the Evans's farm to comfort them, instead?'

Judy prowled up and down, then saw the time and said, 'Hey, we must fly! We've been ages. Oh, I don't know – maybe I'll phone Mr Norris and he'll – oh, I don't know.'

In the end she talked to the Evans' family on the telephone during her lunch break. She found it so unbelievably hard to concentrate. Her lunch was early, but surely, surely Linda and that young naval officer should be out of the theatre now?

Various possibilities shot through her brain. She tried to keep them reasonable. She didn't know, she told herself, how long such an operation took. There might have been complications with the young man *(not with Linda, oh, no, not with Linda)* and his operation may have put the whole list back. In the end, Judy couldn't bear it and went back to the telephone to call Edward Norris.

'I'm waiting for the result from theatre,' she said. 'Is it awful of me to want you to talk to me?'

He was delighted. He told her about other cases, recounted to him by Philip, cases carefully selected by him as having been successful. 'I don't know about your cousin's operation – Philip hasn't said much about that, but I imagine it will be interesting,' he told her, in a matter-of-fact voice that might have been discussing a new composer or the weather. By the time he had got round to describing the taste of the new dish his cook had prepared for him, it reminded her that she hadn't had her own lunch, but she felt very much better. She told him so.

'But you weren't like this last night,' he said gently. 'Has anything else happened?' She told him about Sheila and the young farmer.

They weren't supposed to use the telephone for so long. She explained and hastily rang off, neatly side-stepping another invitation from him. It was all very well; whatever he said by way of comfort, there should have been some news by now.

She decided to take the law into her own hands and go up to the theatre. At least she may be in time to see someone come out, and to judge by their faces whether all was well or not.

It was very quiet on that floor and the light wasn't on outside the theatre. Her heart started beating so fast, it almost suffocated her. No operation was in progress. They were cleaning up in there!

As she stood there, frozen to the spot, wondering what on earth had happened, she heard one theatre nurse say to the other, 'Well, it was the last thing he expected – you could see that! What she'll say when she hears, I shudder to think! I mean, that sort of throat operation–'

And the other girl said, 'When was the last time we had a D.O.T.?'

D.O.T. Dead on the table. Died during the operation. So that was what had happened! Judy slid quietly to the floor.

When she came to, Philip Addison was bending over her. It was an empty side ward, apparently. He had had her head ducked between her knees. He turned to wet a towel and came back and wiped her face with it. That's better!' he approved. 'Had no lunch, I suppose, and came up here snooping. Just what happened to make you go out like a light?'

'Linda's dead, isn't she? You don't have to pretend.'

The corners of his mouth turned down in disapproval about something. So that was what she had heard! He said shortly, 'She's fine, as a matter of fact. I hope she stays that way until she's over it, before some clot of a nurse starts gossiping about him.' He raised his eyes. 'I am no more pleased about a D.O.T. than anyone else, but he had a complication I wasn't prepared for – he quietly passed out under the anaesthetic.'

'Nigel!' Judy gasped. 'So that's what she meant, Oh, no – Linda's in love with him! Really in love with him!'

That didn't please him, either. He pulled her to her feet. 'When did you eat last?' he asked abruptly.

'Oh, I don't know. Breakfast, I think. I didn't eat anything with my coffee.'

'Just as I thought! I'll get permission and take you out to lunch. Yes, I insist. I imagine Home Sister will, too. You look terrible. Judy, don't argue – if you stay here you'll struggle to see your cousin and I don't want her upset. Judy, think! Think what will happen if she is!'

Judy couldn't think that. She knew, as sure as she was standing there being talked to like that by Philip Addison, that the minute Linda came to she would shout for Judy, and then she would shout for Judy to bring her Nigel to her, and when it wasn't done Linda would just shout and shout. She was like that.

Even then it didn't penetrate what he was trying to tell her. The sheer force of his personality urged her to pull herself together, go down to the Nurses' Home to change and to go out to lunch with him. It was unreal, all of it, but he made her keep going, doing what he told her. And he talked – not about the operations that morning but about Edward Norris, and he discussed the telephone call Judy had had with Norris. He discussed the chances of the young farmer, too. 'He'll be all right. He won't lose his legs, if that's what you're worried about, but when he'll walk again, is another question.

But don't tell your friend Sheila – and that is an order!'

An order! The pattern of things to come, where Philip was concerned. He was the boss; both in his work and in Judy's life, and as the days went by, she accepted it.

She let him take her out to lunch whenever he could, and she leaned hard on him to give her courage and strength in the difficult days that followed where Linda was concerned. Linda wouldn't keep quiet. She was a most difficult patient. But Philip produced a measure of restraint in her, by talking to Linda. Linda wouldn't accept Nigel's death when she at last found out, by guessing, and she went to pieces and had to be under sedation and again Philip had to have a quiet talk with her. His personality shaped the lives of the cousins so that any other speculation about them faded into the past, and was replaced by the question: which of them would get Philip Addison?

One day Judy ran into Richard Cartwright. He grinned cheerfully at her and said, 'Well, how tricks? You don't look much the worse for all you've been through, Judy!'

She gaped at him. She just couldn't believe it. She had accepted the way he managed to keep out of sight and sound of her, and the slick way he managed to be deaf, dumb and blind when he met her by accident on the ward. But to act like this now, when the trouble was almost over, was too much for her. She said, 'Do you really want to know how I am, Rick?' and he had the grace to redden.

'Oh, come on, now, Judy! You know me! Avoid trouble! Much the best way! For everyone, wouldn't you say?'

She stood silently, trying to work out what sort of doctor he would be in the future. How could a man be a good doctor when he had this fatal gift for sliding out of anything difficult or embarrassing? She was young enough and idealist enough to think of a good doctor in the shape of the old family GP who had attended her aunt before she died, and she thought of a good surgeon as someone like Philip, who cared so much about each and every patient. Looking at Richard now, it hit her blindingly that he would be destined for a niche in life that required charm (of which he had plenty) and a lot of money to get himself launched. It would be a fashionable clinic she supposed.

She nodded in answer to his question, because she had lost interest. This was only the shell of the man she had loved. There was nothing inside the shell, and she felt cheated, lost and alone, and unconsciously yearning a little more each day towards Philip Addison. He was there all the time, life-sized, ready for her to turn to when she needed help of any kind; as yet unembellished with romantic covering, he was still in her view the good solid friend, but he was, even in that humble guise, rapidly filling the place that Rick had possessed, though she didn't know it.

Rick himself started the process of making her aware of it, in the next few minutes. Nettled that her eyes no longer lit up at the sight of him, he said, 'Well, you'll be soon rid of your sick-room visiting, won't you? Linda's coming on fine, so I hear, so you'll be in circulation again, so what about a date?'

She was astonished that he should suggest such a thing and it showed in her face. Even more nettled, he said, 'Well, surely you can see Linda won't want you sitting by her bedside much longer, now she's developed a nice new bedside friend?'

'What's that supposed to mean?' she asked, wondering who could be visiting Linda, that she herself hadn't been told about. It was true that Linda had now stopped fretting for Nigel. But who? Were they letting Felix Morford go up and see her? She dismissed that thought almost at once, although Felix was beginning to get about the ward in a wheel chair, now his spinal operation had been such a success. Get them about to get the blood moving, that was the new belief and practice.

Rick took her by the shoulders and shook her gently. 'What's the matter with you? You're not really paying attention to me, are you? I'm talking of Addison, of course! Didn't you know? My dear, what good is the grapevine with someone like you who doesn't even listen? He's even been seen popping into her room late at night – oh, I tell you, that girl could twist any chap round her little finger! Except old Rick ... I'm foolproof.'

Her head swam a little, but she took a hold on herself. He was cross about something, or he wouldn't say such a thing about Philip. And Philip wouldn't do such a thing anyway. 'Foolproof?' she echoed. 'Well, maybe, Rick, but you're also only half alive. You run away from experiencing emotion, so how can you pat yourself on the back? You've nothing to pat yourself on the back for!' and she marched away, feeling curiously flat, empty again. In hospital, when something is said about someone the gossip seems so much more insidious than outside, because the world of hospital is a tight little sealed-in world that is not quite comparable with outside. Judy trusted Philip, and yet ... and yet there just might be something in what Rick said, allowing for the way Rick could make things seem different to what they were. Philip might have been called late to Linda's room, but not to sit there with her and have jolly intimate chats. But the thought persisted. People were talking of Linda's quick way of 'getting over' Nigel's death, as if someone else had already taken his place. Linda herself no longer lay there with tears welling out of her eyes, constantly fretting for that young man. She was beginning to be 'alive' again inside her; there was a gleam in her eyes again, as there always had been when she made a new conquest. Ill as she was, and not allowed to use that beautiful voice for fear of damaging it by using it too soon, she could still think of men and where she fitted into the scene of their admiration.

Well, it could be Maurice Timbrell, she supposed, but that afternoon on the Men's Ward, she learned from the little they said, that it wasn't Maurice – he was trying to probe and find out how long she herself was going to stay in the world of nursing.

'Mr Timbrell, you aren't suggesting you think I could *act?*'

'I know dashed well you could, Judy. What's more, I think you have everything I need, so if you get fed up with this dreary existence, you just get in touch with me,' and he insisted on giving her his card.

'But it's my cousin Linda who is interested in the stage, and it's Linda who has the singing voice,' Judy said, straightening his bed-clothes for the third time in the last hour. She was so intent on the task that she didn't notice the sharp look he directed up at her, but he said nothing.

Felix Morford merely smiled at her when she got round to his bed. He hadn't asked about Linda for two days.

'How are you?' she wrote on his pad.

'Worried,' he said briefly.

'Why?' she wrote, turning sympathetic brown eyes full on him.

He shrugged. 'Two more operations before the one on my ears – another six months, if not more, spent in here!'

'Well, it will soon go,' she wrote. 'And think how you'll feel when it's all over, and you're fit again!'

'*If* I'm fit,' he corrected her. 'And *if* it's any use being fit.'

'Now why do you say that?'

'I can't keep pace with your cousin Linda,' he admitted. 'I only heard today about the chap she cared about, who didn't come out of theatre. I didn't even know she knew him. And now she's got someone else.'

'No, that isn't true,' Judy wrote. 'I would have heard of him, and I haven't.'

'No, you wouldn't,' Felix said. 'You'd be the last to hear, my dear.'

She looked so shocked, he put his hand on hers. 'Have you anyone in your life?'

'Well, no, but I'm training to be a nurse,' she wrote on the pad, and now it was full, and she tried to tear the page off to throw it away after he had read it but he wouldn't let her. He said, 'I'd like to keep the denial you've written about your cousin, in case it's true. It would help if I thought I stood a ghost of a chance with her,' he said sadly.

Judy was kind and cheerful most of the time, but when a wave of anger washed over her, she looked a different person. She swept past Rick who had come on the ward to see one patient at the end of the ward, and even the self-satisfied Rick could see that Judy honestly hadn't noticed him.

'Well, what's the matter with her?' he asked the ward at large. The Staff Nurse looked scornfully at him and didn't answer but Maurice Timbrell said, 'She's just heard that her cousin Linda has got someone else in tow.'

'So? I told her that myself not so long ago and she didn't believe me!' Rick said frowning.

Maurice shrugged as if to say that Judy wouldn't. 'Sunshine boy here has told her,' he said, nodding to Felix Morford, who had his eyes closed, 'and she believes him.'

'She ought to be pleased,' Rick said, losing interest. 'She didn't want Addison herself, did she?'

Maurice Timbrell looked scornfully at him this time. Rick said cheerfully, 'Oh well, if she did, she should have been smarter off the mark. She's lost him now. Her cousin Linda never lets go when she wants something.'

That thought nagged at Judy, and wouldn't go, no matter how much she willed herself to make it vanish. The next time she saw Philip, she decided to put it to the test. After all, he was asking her to go for a short drive, in the two free hours she had. She said, 'Don't you want to sit with Linda?'

'No, she's calm at the moment,' he said. 'Let's get some fresh air, which you look as if you need.'

There was no way, Judy thought, of discovering which of them he liked most, but the chances were that he was being kind to Judy because she was the only relative of Linda. He would always keep them both happy. He was that sort of man.

But she couldn't leave it alone. In the car, she said, 'You like Linda now, don't you?'

Never had he been more tempted to say that Linda was the one and only patient he didn't like and had never liked and never would. He hadn't found one endearing quality in Linda. She hadn't even much courage. He thought of ivy clinging to a tree and killing it, and hated himself for the analogy. She was dear to Judy and somehow he must not only make it sound as if he liked Linda but he must make it convincing.

'Linda is,' he smiled, 'a challenge. I've

always loved a challenge. Do you know I can make her even stop trying to talk? That, you must admit, is rather an achievement.'

Judy thought about it, and decided he had fallen under Linda's spell and was trying to play it down, because he had been Judy's friend from the first and no great admirer of Linda and he was the sort of man who might be ashamed at such a quick change in his affections. 'Yes, Oh yes, I must admit that,' she said, in a small voice.

It was such a short drive that night. He had to get back to see a patient. As they got out of the car, in the car park, he was struck with the silence, the calm of the starspangled night sky, the subdued murmur of the busy streets some way away. It was rather soothing, and perhaps what he had been looking for, as a quiet place to tell her what he had been thinking. There was rarely a quiet place to talk unless he pulled the car into a layby, which rather smacked of the younger people and the way they conducted their romantic talks. He wondered how he should begin, and had actually said, 'Judy, I want to tell—' when he heard running footsteps and a voice said, 'I'm sure I saw Mr Addison's car come in!' The man had a torch. It was one of the porters. Philip was wanted: it was an emergency.

Judy didn't know whether to be relieved or disappointed. He had been going to say he wanted to tell her something. What else but that he had, at long last, succumbed to Linda's personality? They all did. Even poor Felix Morford.

She watched him hurry back after having seen her to the door of the Nurses' Home. Where were his thoughts now? What was Linda thinking, lying up there in isolation?'

Now Judy had to know. The next time she saw her cousin, she formed her own conclusion. Linda was bright-eyed, already looking a lot better. She wrote punctiliously on the provided pad, 'Philip says I can get up soon!' and during that short visit she wrote 'Philip says' or 'Philip thinks' or 'Philip has arranged' with a delight and persistence that left Judy in no doubt as to what was happening under her nose.

When she left her cousin's room, she asked herself: did she mind? Did she really mind Linda drawing Philip to her like a bud being drawn to open to the sunshine? Wasn't it always what happened? And had Philip shown more than friendship for herself, that she should feel so dispossessed? She was ashamed, and a little breathless with a sort of horror that she should mind. After all, Linda married to Philip would be much less of an anxiety than Linda married to almost anybody else.

But she did mind and it wasn't a bit of use trying to tell herself that she didn't. But she wouldn't let herself dwell on the matter to find out how much she minded. That way lay disaster.

Chapter Eleven

But she must get herself interested in something else. Or someone. Philip watched her from a distance; she seemed to be in a fever, taking on anyone else's duty in her spare time, running errands for the patients, just keeping going every waking minute, as if she had made a pact with herself not to allow herself time to think. Philip couldn't understand it.

The following day Edward Norris's man telephoned her. 'If you've got a minute, nurse, to come over and cheer the guvnor up, I'd be much obliged, personally obliged, I really would. I know you've got precious little spare time, especially these days, but if you could spare say an hour, I'd come over and pick you up, *and* take you back.'

'But of course I'll come,' Judy said warmly. 'Whose idea is this? Mr Norris's or yours?'

'I heard him say he'd like to hear you play, nurse, but since then you've not been here and the piano's been shut up. I don't know why.'

Judy thought quickly, and told him briskly he could call for her after lunch. There was a whole long afternoon stretching its elongated hours. She couldn't see Linda, who had the surgeons looking at her today, and she couldn't see Sheila either. Thelma had made it up with the Casualty Officer and was sporting a very modest little diamond ring on a cord round her neck, so there was nobody here, except Rick, who persevered with his asking her to go out with him simply because he couldn't understand how one person could hold out against him for so long.

Edward Norris was so pleased when she arrived. 'I didn't think you'd come,' he said, sincerely.

'Why not? Philip is with the other top brass, with my cousin Linda, so I have lots of time on my hands. Besides, I think he's falling a little in love with my cousin Linda. Everybody does, you know.'

Edward's ears were attuned to things in a person's voice that perhaps other people didn't hear. He said, 'You and I are going to cheer each other up. You are going to be good for me. Do you know that? Now, first of all, we'll explore the town. You don't know Oakmere, do you?'

Judy thought he meant they were to be driven about, but it wasn't like that at all. Edward walked about the town with her and pointed out things as if he had eyes to see. 'I've always loved this town. It's one of the few gems left, unhurt by progress – of course, I do a lot towards that. I write a great deal in the press about it, and I put my hand in my pocket towards things to help such as the Norris Park for children, over there!'

He pointed with his stick but at that time there were no children. 'How did you–?' she began, then bit her lip remembering Philip's warning.

Edward was very pleased to be able to tell her how he knew where he was. 'I could tell you every stick and stone of this town because when I first lost my sight I used to go about counting. Not to be able to get about on my own would have plunged me into the depths of despair. I think I always knew that in spite of Philip's skill as a surgeon and in spite of his wealth of big names of specialists on which to call, nobody could do anything for me. Well, I accepted that. I believe in accepting everything – I never fight unless its against injustice, and then I fight like a savage. And I mean that! Injustice really makes me see red.'

'Oh, I can't believe that! You're such a gentle person!' Judy said warmly.

'Well, if you like to believe that of me, I shan't argue with you, my dear. Perhaps you'll believe it a little later on when you know me better. I suppose I fought like a savage, to replace my sight with other things. I have numerous mechanical devices which help.'

'Now that's interesting!' Judy exclaimed. 'Tell me!'

'Well, when anyone telephones me, I have the conversation taped, so that I can consider it afterwards, either as to the content of the conversation or the nuances of that voice. I have a sound recorder of people's footsteps. And I take sound recordings of animals and birds. Purely for interest, but in a way it's helped me to get about. You'd never believe how a whisper of sound can be an explosion to a person without sight, whereas those who can see might not notice it.'

'And I suppose you'll tape my playing on your piano, to see how many mistakes I make,' Judy laughed.

'I shall tape your playing so that I can hear it when you're not with me,' he corrected her.

His companionship was as silk-smooth and polished as the rest of his manner. Judy didn't know whether she liked it or not. She was bedevilled by too many memories of Philip Addison, which puzzled her. Most of the time she had spent with him, she had been thinking about Rick or grieving about Rick. How, then, could Philip have imposed his personality on her, in spite of that?

Hearing Judy play on tape, however, proved a hollow pleasure to Edward, and he came to look forward to her being with him for some part of every day. The nurses in the First Year worked on a block system, so that their long tiring day was split in the middle. That gave her three hours free, and Edward's man fetched her and drove her back to the hospital on time.

Philip stopped her one day when she had just returned from hearing Edward's newest additions to his hi-fi equipment. 'Judy, where have you been?' he asked.

'Linda! She's worse!' Judy exclaimed, a hand flying to her throat, and her colour fading.

For once, Philip lost patience. 'Oh, for heavens sake, do you think I would tell you such a thing in that way? Linda's all right, and you are to stop worrying about her!'

Because you are there to do the worrying now, Judy found herself thinking, so she just nodded and stood thinking, wondering what she should tell him. It was none of his business now, of course, and in a queer way she didn't want anyone to know about the treasured hours she spent with Edward. Although not sure of how she felt about him, they were treasured hours nonetheless, because somehow he provided an escape for her from the tensions of her private life at the hospital. So she said, 'I just go out, Philip. It's all right. I'm allowed to in my free time.'

He looked rather taken aback. 'You mean you don't want to tell me where you go and what you do?'

'No, I don't mean that I don't want to exactly. I just don't see why you should be bothered. You've been very kind to me in the past, but now all your free time is taken up with Linda, so you don't need to worry about me.'

'What's that supposed to mean?'

'I mean, it's perfectly all right, sir. And I must go now – I'm back on duty.'

'Then I'll walk up to the ward with you and talk on the way because that last remark makes no sense at all to me and there was something I wanted to say to you. I started to, that night in the car park, and I don't seem to have found an appropriate moment since, to coincide with being able to find you, Judy!'

'I know what you were going to say, Philip, and I'm only too glad, since it's making Linda so happy, and she's always talking about you–'

Unfortunately he was thinking about what he wanted to say to Judy at the time, and he missed the full import of all that until she had gone. She did it very neatly, sidestepping so that Matron and another surgeon could walk between them, and the surgeon turned round and buttonholed Philip while Judy escaped. Philip was furious.

When he got free from his colleague, he went up to see Linda. She was just waking up, and looked very sleepy and cuddly. Her hair was tumbled from the way she churned about on her pillows, into thick silky ringlets, but it suited her, better than the sophisticated styles she had experimented with before her illness. Her eyes widened at the sight of him and she held out her hand to him.

His anger was held in check. They had worked too hard on this patient to have him throw everything away in shouting at her. So he didn't say what he had been going to. In any case, you couldn't reason with Linda when she was fit and well, so it was no use trying to reason with her now. He pulled out the stool and sat by her, but she made an evasive movement so he shouldn't take her pulse, and grabbed his hand instead. She had white, clinging little hands, and she liked to play at hiding one inside the large hollow his made, and folding his fingers over so that nothing of her hand could be seen. But he wouldn't play today.

She wrote on her pad: 'Cross? Who with? Me?'

He shook his head, so she wrote: 'Who, then?' but he pushed the pad away and asked her instead, 'Do you know where Judy goes in her spare time?'

She wrote busily: 'Rick?' and as Philip's brow grew thunderous, she wrote, with a half-apologetic look, 'Well, they're both crazy about boats and swimming.' And she watched him.

Philip had other things on his mind. 'Morford. Have they told you how he's getting on?' which made Linda rather sulky because she hadn't wanted him to think of other things; she wanted to watch his reactions about the suggestion that Judy had gone back to Richard Cartwright.

She shrugged. 'Who cares?' she wrote.

'Don't be naughty. He's a very nice chap and he asks all the time about you. I was thinking it would be kind if you wrote a little note to him, wishing him well. It would help me,' he murmured, 'in the sense that my patient would become happy in time for his next operation.'

'That's different!' Linda wrote, and scribbled a note on a clean sheet. 'Dear Mr Morford, The ginger nurse hopes you are doing fine. Keep your fingers crossed – I'm sure it will work out all right.'

'Now sign it – Linda Lawrence,' Philip gently ordered.

He looked as if he were going to have trouble. Linda hadn't wanted to write the note anyway, and she had managed to make it sound like Judy. Philip said, 'If you want me to come back again, you sign that "Linda Lawrence" and look sharp about it,' so after a tussle with herself, she signed it and thrust it at him. On her own pad she wrote: 'Kiss me!'

'Certainly not!' he said coolly and went out with the note for Felix Morford. Leaving Linda inclined to giggle, because she chose to read into those two words of his that he would if the place and opportunity were right.

Felix Morford studied the note with exaggerated care, when Philip gave it to him. The man was struggling not to be pleased and hopeful, he could see.

'Well?' Philip said, smiling at him, forgetting Felix couldn't hear him.

Felix said, 'How is that beautiful voice, Mr Addison?'

That was not the sort of question Philip relished just then. He wrote on the pad held out to him, 'She has not been allowed to try it yet, naturally. It's early days. The scar is healing nicely on her throat. It will fade in time.' And with that, Felix had to be content.

Philip waited while he struggled with a note for Linda, but in the end, Felix gave it up, and shrugged helplessly. 'I – don't know what to say to her,' he choked. 'What can I say in a few words on this size sheet?'

'Of course you can't,' Philip wrote on his pad. 'But how about writing a letter?' That should keep Felix Morford busy and mentally occupied until the next morning when they would rush his ear operation on him.

197

And then, depending on failure or success, it was in the lap of the gods. But if Linda didn't get interested in Felix Morford, Philip had an uncomfortable feeling that she would fasten those clinging little hands on to himself, aided and abetted by the devoted Judy.

But as he left the ward he asked himself again, why should Judy feel like that now? He had been almost certain that she was more than friendly towards himself that last time they had been out together. The closeness of the bond between them had been so obvious that he had been emboldened to speak to her about themselves, when he could manage to stop her talking about Cartwright and her cousin Linda. Emboldened? Well, perhaps if he had been just that, he told himself scornfully, something good might come out of it. As it was, he had hesitated, and lost the opportunity.

He forgot that he had half promised Linda to go back to her ward. She was waiting for him, and worked herself up into a passion of anger and indignation because he hadn't come. She asked the nurse who came in with her tea, where he was. That nurse had just seen him come out of the ward Judy was on. He had been looking for Judy. Judy was in the kitchen, heating some milk, and he had gone in. The nurse had noticed particularly the warmth of his smile for Judy, and wondered a little. Philip Addison usually behaved as if nurses were rather intelligent schoolgirls who had to be kept out of trouble by him, in the guise of a friendly uncle. He wasn't looking uncle-ish at Judy. But there was no sense in letting Linda know that, so she said, 'Couldn't say, m'dear. I expect he'll be along later,' and signalled to the junior the other side of the bed to get out before she decided to say something.

The junior, who had been mopping up Linda's fruit drink she had managed to spill, hadn't seen the question Linda had written down, so she looked rather blankly at her senior signalling her to keep quiet. Linda noticed, however, and held up the paper she had written the question on. The junior reddened and stuttered 'What am I supposed to say? You *do* know where he is!'

'Oh, do take that rag back to the kitchen before it drips all over the bed,' the other nurse said wearily, but Linda wasn't going to be fobbed off like that. She just remembered in time not to speak, but her hand flew out and fastened on to the junior's wrist, and she pinched her so the girl squealed.

'Okay, I'll tell you – I don't know what all the fuss is about. He was only with your own cousin – what's it matter? It's all in the family, isn't it?'

Philip, having elicited the information at

last from Judy that she had been that day to see his friend Edward Norris, went back to Linda's room with mixed feelings and found an unwelcome scene going on. Linda was sobbing and wailing, and the ward sister and a junior doctor trying to quieten her before she forgot the don't talk rule.

Philip said wearily, 'Oh, do shut up, Linda! What's the trouble about, Sister?'

'I don't know, Mr Addison,' the sister said heatedly, 'but I gather a junior nurse said something tactless—'

'About where you were, sir,' the junior houseman put in, which didn't help matters.

Philip said smoothly, 'I told you I'd be back, didn't I, Linda? Meantime I went to find Judy, to ask her what she did with her spare hours and if she could manage to spend a little more time with you. That's all, and here I am, as I promised!'

Suddenly the scene was over, and everybody breathed again because in spite of everything, Linda had broken the rules and used her voice. There were five more days to go, before she could do that. Philip was left in there with her, with the door open.

He mopped her eyes, and noticed how little she had impaired her complexion. Now she was smiling, gratified, not a little unpleased with the fuss she could cause. This had been almost as enjoyable as the meeting of the top brass round her bed. And now she had Philip back, as promised.

She wrote on her pad, 'Don't want Judy. Only want you. Besides, why spoil Judy's fun with – whoever she's out with?'

'You said Rick, I believe,' Philip said coolly, tearing off the sheet and crumpling it into a ball with unnecessary violence. 'As it happens, it wasn't Cartwright at all, nor has it been, ever – not since you got ill. Now I wonder what made you think it was?'

'She doesn't tell me anything,' Linda wrote, her face crumpling.

'Then I will tell you where she gets to,' Philip said softly. 'She goes to play the piano to a blind ex-patient of mine, at my request. I only asked her to, the once, but being Judy, and very generous, she kept it up because she liked it. Now, aren't you just a little ashamed?'

For reasons of her own, she nodded. 'Why do you come and sit by me, considering you don't like me at all?' she wrote.

Philip could tease in a big-brotherly way if he felt like it. 'No idea,' he said now, with a broad grin.

Linda scowled. 'When can I say something?' she wrote fiercely.

'You know when, to the day, and you love yourself much too much to wreck the chances of keeping that beautiful voice,' he said calmly. 'Now do let's conduct a rational if one-sided conversation, my dear girl, because there's something I want to ask you.' He smiled encouragingly at her. 'When's Judy's birthday?'

She was so shocked, that her face literally contorted with rage and jealousy. She wasn't even aware of it, until Philip slowly sat up, staring at her. She quickly smiled, nodded, and wrote a date down on her pad. A date a week ago.

'Oh, I've missed it. I thought it was somewhere around this date,' he said, and sounded so disappointed, Linda could have thrown the water-jug at him. But she was in command of herself again, and smiled sadly at him, shrugging. Now she was waiting for him to ask when hers was, until she remembered he had only to move his hand to find it, on her notes, so it wasn't any use faking it.

'Never mind, not to worry. It was just a thought,' Philip said, getting up. All his mind was on Judy now, being fetched and brought back by Edward's chauffeur, and charming a man who had so much to offer her, so much charm to offer it with, so much time in which to charm her. He wondered hopelessly why he had ever taken Judy to see Edward in the first place. He said casually to Linda, 'So long, poppet – back tomorrow, if possible.'

It was his usual way of saying goodbye. He had never been guilty of making a goodbye

that could in any way have been miscon-
strued by anyone, least of all Linda herself,
as tender. Even when she was very ill, he
had been casual, if only to persuade her that
she was less ill than she was. So he really
wasn't prepared for her to violently shake
her head and grovel for her pad and pencil
among the again tumbled bedclothes.

But now he wanted to see Judy again. 'Not
now, Linda – must go! Write me a note next
time,' he said, and strode to the door.

Linda was equally sure he was going to
find Judy, and it was her undoing. The ward
sister heard her roar at him in her office and
joined the others who came running. 'NO!
DON'T GO, PHILIP!' And the sound of
that voice alone, rooted him to the spot,
horrified.

Chapter Twelve

Edward touched Judy's face and found it damp. 'You've been crying and you've deserted me for four whole days. I don't know how to ask you what's happened.'

'My cousin Linda,' she said. 'I don't know what to do. Oh no, she's not dead, and she isn't unwell, but she forgot and used her voice before the appointed day to try it. She didn't even just speak – she shouted, they tell me. Some of the women on the general ward said they even heard what she said!'

'And she's ruined everything?' Edward asked gently, pushing Judy down in to an armchair near him.

Judy could hardly speak. 'We haven't even a tape of her voice as it used to be. It was like velvet, and such a lovely singing voice. Oh, why did it have to happen?'

Edward didn't answer. He had heard a curt recital of what happened from Philip and he had also heard from Philip the result of his operation on Felix Morford. Philip took it badly when things went wrong in his operating theatre. This was a bitter double blow for him. Felix Morford's hearing hadn't been restored.

'Well, never mind, Judy. At least your cousin has her surgeon to comfort her, at least, so I gather.'

'From whom?' she asked in surprise.

'From you, of course. You've given me to understand that Philip spends every minute he can with her, and that your cousin talks about him in a proprietary manner.'

'Oh, I see. Yes, I thought perhaps Philip had said something to you about it.'

'No, I don't have Philip visit me nowadays,' Edward said carefully. He meant he hadn't spoken with Philip since the day he had brought Judy to meet him, a day when he had thought Philip and Judy were both in love. He listened, straining every faculty to try and understand from the nuances in Judy's voice, what had gone wrong.

'Judy, would you tell me something? As a friend?' he pleaded. 'I shouldn't ask it but I want to help you. Who do you care for most – which man – at the moment? I mean, is it Philip, or is it still this Dr Cartwright that I hear so much about?'

'Oh, Edward, not you too! That's all people talk about – being in love! I'm worried, and grieved, and I feel inadequate because people close to me are in trouble and I can't help. My cousin Linda–'

'–she comes first, I take it?' Edward murmured.

'I don't know, Edward, I don't know,' Judy

fretted, getting up. 'She is very close. So is Philip – we're good friends. At least, we were. Then when I thought my cousin Linda had fallen in love with him and he with her, well, I just tried to cut it off – he won't want me claiming friendship with him when there's Linda. And she's unhappy for her voice – she loved singing. And he's not happy because he couldn't do more for her. And poor Felix Morford is in love with my cousin Linda and he doesn't know when he'll be out of hospital. And I, who have no problems of my own, I have excellent health and everything is going well with me.'

'Is it?' he asked gently. 'Now I would have thought that you were quietly suffering as much grief and frustration as the others only you don't make such a fuss about how you feel.' But she wouldn't answer that, so he pursued, 'Philip – did he tell you he was in love with your cousin Linda, in so many words?'

She laughed shortly. 'I don't suppose he knows. But he talks about her all the time and he goes up to her room whenever he can – how much more do I have to know, to convince me?'

'And your cousin Linda – I thought she was in love with the young naval officer who infected her with this illness.'

Judy agreed with that. 'He's dead,' she said shortly. 'And meantime Philip has been so good to Linda, and Linda must have some-one to shower with her affection and charm.'

He sighed. 'So you are pretty sure that Philip will finish up as the husband of your cousin Linda. Will she continue nursing, do you suppose?'

'I don't know! She's in such a state over her voice. It was a quite exceptional voice, her speaking voice, too,' Judy said.

'So is yours ... quite exceptional.' Edward said. 'I have to rely on my finger-tips to know what your face is like, and other people's descriptions to know what your colouring is, but your voice, and what your hands can do on the piano – ah, those I can decide for myself, and I am in love with both.'

It wasn't the time or place, and she was merely embarrassed. 'You don't know what you really like, while you're in this world of darkness,' she said passionately. 'If there was something new cropping up tomorrow in the world of surgery, which would give you back your sight, you might find that you couldn't think why you had liked my voice. It's not a true test.'

He stood regarding her, though his eyes couldn't see her. It was uncanny, the way he acted as if he could see. A tall elegant man with an amused half smile playing around the corners of his mouth. 'Don't tell me I'm like a child, not knowing what I want,' he said gently. 'I know very well what I want. I want to hear your voice around me, I want your personality, your very real interest in everything I say and do – in short, I want you, Judy. I am asking you to marry me.'

'Oh, Edward, don't do any such thing!' she said, an upset note in her voice. 'You haven't known me long enough – you don't know anything about me! Besides–'

'Besides, your cousin Linda hasn't met me, and might decide she wanted me herself?' he drawled. 'Judy, don't lose your temper with me! I can see through people better than people can with eyes to see. I haven't even met your cousin, but I know her through the things you and Philip and other people have said. She's charming and gay and selfish and utterly unprincipled.' He took both her hands in his, as if he could see them. 'Judy, face it! Face it! By her very nature, she'll wreck your life! All right you both grew up together! I imagine from what I know of you that you just gave in to her every whim. But you can't do that any more, because men friends are involved. It isn't the same as when you were both at school.'

He made his voice heard above hers, and finally she stopped trying to shout him down, because clearly he had his own ideas about Linda and didn't want to hear her defending her cousin. Judy kept quiet, and finally he said, 'Well, now, I've said enough about this very dear cousin of yours to wreck my own chances with you, haven't I?'

'No. No, of course not. Don't be silly. It's just that you don't know her. When you've met her, got to know her, you'll see how wrong you were.'

'I hope you're right, Judy,' he said grimly. 'But it's a hazard any chap has to take, where you're concerned. In marrying you, one takes on a load of mischief as well.'

'But that's what Rick said!' she whispered, appalled.

'This Dr Cartwright?'

She nodded, then remembering he couldn't see, she said, 'Yes, and I thought Rick was cruel and unkind to Linda. But you're not cruel and unkind. Oh, I can only think that she doesn't let her best be seen—'

'Judy, if you don't take the blinkers off your eyes soon, you won't have a life left to enjoy, I can assure you!' Edward said.

Now that Linda's voice had been tried, she was swiftly got up on to her feet. She protested, said she wasn't well enough, but Philip was her surgeon and he said there was no reason for her to stay in bed, and that private room was needed for someone else. She was taken out on the balcony in the sunshine, and then she gravitated to the patient's garden, protesting every inch of the way and using every ruse she could, to stay and hide in her room.

'I'm ill and you don't care,' she sobbed,

but Philip wasn't one to be intimidated. 'Besides, I don't want anyone to hear this horribly scratchy voice you've left me with!'

'It was your own fault,' he retorted. 'If you hadn't been in a temper with me, and shouted, it wouldn't have happened!'

'It was your fault for walking out on me!' she roared.

'The more you do that, Linda, the worse your voice will be,' he told her, very seriously. 'Now, you are going to get fully dressed today and go down the corridor for a walk.'

'No, no, I won't! You're heartless! You must know very well I'm in love with you! Why do I have to beg you to kiss me? Never in my life have I had to beg a man to do that before!'

'I'll tell you why, Linda,' Philip said quietly, taking her by the shoulders in a firm grip she couldn't evade. 'Now is the time for you to know that I am not the man to fall for your little wiles and tricks. I am not in love with you, and I'm not having you make things awkward for me or for Judy, by letting you make the situation get out of hand. Understand me?'

'What's Judy got to do with it?' she whispered, appalled.

'My dear, you fall in and out of love like a kitten falling in and out of its basket, but Judy isn't like that, and Judy is the one I am interested in. So don't let me hear your demanding to be kissed, not any more. Understood?'

'*Judy?*' Linda couldn't believe it. She hadn't taken much notice of Judy going around with him at first because she had wanted Rick. She had tried Philip herself but he had been difficult to get worked up over, but then Judy hadn't seemed to want him. Rick had been the bone of contention. And then she had met Nigel. Judy hadn't even known about Nigel. Linda hugged the memory of Nigel to her, and thought with rage that Judy had managed somehow to capture this man who had never seemed interesting to Linda, but who had somehow blossomed under Judy's influence. Now she wanted him and must have him.

'Yes, Judy. Now come on, there's a good girl. I'm waiting.'

With a nurse on one side and Philip on the other, Linda made her first sortie among people, hating the quick glance they gave her, until the nurse said, 'It's your hair! It's so trendy! Everyone's jealous!' That comforted her to some extent. And nobody seemed surprised about her new voice. She forgot that most people had heard that first roar when Linda had been angry and weren't at all surprised at the result. The first little walk was such a success that she was ordered to sit in the patient's garden every afternoon so long as it was fine.

'I will if Judy stays with me,' she said,

tight-lipped.

Judy received this summons with her usual willingness but Edward was very angry when he heard. 'I don't mind your being with her every other afternoon, but don't desert me altogether!' he said, surprise mingling with his indignation.

Linda said, instinct telling her that Judy was bothered, 'I wonder where you go in the afternoons, that this should put you out so much? Oh yes, it does put you out– I know you! This is just duty, isn't it? I bet Philip told you you had to sit with me. Confess it!'

'Well, yes, he did, but it isn't duty. I have wanted to be with you but they kept making me go out to get fresh air.'

'Where did you go?' Linda asked, looking away, as if she weren't very much interested.

'Sometimes to the town, sometimes to Jennetts Cross–'

'What on earth for?'

'Oh, the island fascinates me, ever since Rick took me there,' Judy said unthinkingly, and then she had to tell Linda all about it. 'But it doesn't matter. It belongs to Philip's family.'

That was something Linda hadn't known. Anger stirred in her to think that Judy should keep so much to herself.

'And where else do you go?' she asked idly.

'Oakmere, sometimes, to see Philip's patient, and sometimes to Skidgate–'

'To see Philip's brother, I suppose,' Linda jeered.

'No. I suppose I should go. They did ask me to go and play – there was some thought of my taking up lessons again. I'd hate to lose my playing.'

'As I've lost my singing!' Linda flared. 'I don't know how you can have all this fun, or tell me about it, when you've got everything and I've got nothing! No, I haven't! I've lost my voice and I've lost the man I loved–'

'Why didn't you tell me about him before, Lin?' Judy asked.

'Because he was mine, mine, and now he's gone,' Linda sobbed. 'And now you're taking away everything else I might have.'

'I don't understand,' Judy gasped. 'What am I taking away?'

'Oh, never mind!' Linda snapped, then she made some attempt to pull herself together, and said, 'I'm a grouch. Sorry. To prove I didn't mean it, I'll ask you to tell me about your love life. There! That proves I'm trying to make amends, doesn't it, because I never wanted to hear about things you said. I always wanted to be the one to do the talking, remember?'

That was true. Judy patted her cousin's hand and said, 'I understand. Well, to be honest, I just haven't got a love-life. Well,' she said blushing, and amending that, under her cousin's keen eye, 'that is to say, *I'm* not

214

in love. Edward did propose to me, but I told him I wasn't the one for him. He's nice. You'd like him,' she said, and looking at her hands, talked at length about Edward Norris and the way he had taught himself to get about so that people didn't know he was blind.

Linda said, carefully controlling her urge to flare out at Judy again, 'Well, if he's youngish and handsome and as well-off as he sounds, aren't you just a little potty in not snapping him up? Rich men don't grow on trees for hard-up little nurses.'

'There's more to marriage than that, Lin, and you know how I feel about it,' Judy said.

'I suppose you really mean you're still in love with Rick!'

'I don't suppose I'll ever get him out of my system,' Judy said slowly. 'At least, not the man I thought he was.' But that was well over Linda's head. To her outraged mind, it meant that Judy was still hanging on to rich Dr Cartwright, while she played with the idea of leading on the rich blind ex-patient, and at the same time kept Philip interested in her, too. Judy's enormities piled themselves up in Linda's mind until she could hardly be civil.

To make matters worse, Philip usually strolled along and sat with Linda when Judy was with her, and got up to go when Judy went – and the following day Rick started doing the same thing. Judy said, when Rick left them, 'That was nice of him. I thought he'd come along and see you. Perhaps he'll visit you tomorrow – well, I must go and see poor Edward Norris – I did promise.'

'Well, don't bother to find a baby-sitter for me!' Linda snapped. 'I daresay, if I asked nicely enough, I could be taken to see Felix Morford. That would be a thrill, wouldn't it?'

Judy was genuinely pleased. 'Oh, what a good idea!' she exclaimed. 'That poor man, he's sure nothing will go right for him and sure he won't ever manage to interest you. You know how much he likes you, Lin, and he isn't hard up either.'

Linda smiled but said nothing.

She did go and visit Felix Morford the next day. Maurice Timbrell's bed was empty, she quickly noticed, and most of the other men had gone, who knew her. She let out a quick sigh of relief. Now nobody would be likely to tell Felix what had happened to her voice and she could play this new game with cleverness.

The nurses were pleased that she had made the effort to visit him, and Felix himself was so delighted, he could hardly speak. Linda was happy to write countless notes and hold them up for him and by degrees he got articulate again. He seemed different. Taller in the bed. She remembered she had

216

only seen him lying down. 'How tall are you when you're standing?' she wrote, forgetting that he might never stand again and that this was a thorny subject.

He told her, 'Six feet in my socks. Why, do you prefer short chaps?'

'Goodness, no! Tall ones, always,' she wrote.

'Linda, go round and say a word to the other chaps, will you?' he asked her. 'I've told them all about you and they want to know you.'

She hesitated. This was not what she wanted, but of course, to please Felix, she must do something like this, or he would remember that only Judy had the generosity to give people her time. So she wrote, 'I'll go and write a message for each – mustn't strain my voice,' and that satisfied him. Linda being charming could be a very charming person indeed, and Felix was pronounced the luckiest dog, after she had gone.

The nurse hadn't come back for her yet. She had been given half an hour, and only stayed fifteen minutes. There was time to make a telephone call, Linda thought.

It wasn't difficult to find Edward Norris's number, or to get it, in one of the booths in the main hall. Judy would still be there, and with a bit of luck she could kill two birds with one stone.

Judy and Edward had been talking about

Linda, and now a silence had fallen. A cosy silence, the sort Edward liked. He was wondering whether he could propose to her again, or just encourage her to talk about this cousin of hers, so that perhaps she would give him a clue how to segregate the girls. He knew, without meeting Linda, that he could never stand her in his otherwise tranquil life.

And then Linda telephoned. Her voice came over the wire harshly. Judy, sitting so near him, heard and recognised Linda's voice outside the instrument, and sprang up in alarm. 'It's your cousin – she wants you to do something for her,' he said, in displeasure.

He listened to the speed with which Judy got to the telephone and the way she answered her cousin. 'Yes, dear, of course I will – but how did it happen? No, I won't wait to ask questions, I'll go. Don't *worry!* Lin, don't *cry!* It will harm your voice! *Trust* me, Lin – don't worry, just leave it to me!'

Judy's one-sided conversation was predictable, he thought, as he waited to hear what it was all about.

Judy looked at him as if she had forgotten his existence. He said, 'What is it, Judy? Your sister is ill again?'

'No, no, but in trouble, desperate trouble! Please don't ask me about it now, Edward! Let me go!'

'Certainly, my dear, if you must, but first let me ring down to my man to get the car out. Well, you'll need transport back to the hospital, won't you?'

Judy said, 'Don't bother, I'll get a cab – it isn't the hospital anyway,' and rushed out.

The very fact that Linda had been in a terrible emotional state was enough to convince Judy that the thing was urgent. She was also acting on the habits of a lifetime; when Linda came to her for help, all the past upsets between them were forgotten – they were close again. Linda was coming to Judy for help. For Judy that was all that mattered.

She had grabbed up her handbag but her coat had been left behind. She didn't know where Edward's man had taken it – he always robbed her of her coat and produced it at going home time. Today she couldn't stop. The sky was heavy with a threatening storm but she was lucky and caught a cab. The taxi man said he could take her to Jennetts Cross, and she said, 'Fast!'

Back in the taxi she had time to think it over. It seemed that Linda felt she had caused the trouble by something she had said, but whether to Philip or to Rick, it hadn't been clear. In Judy's mind the suppressed passions about the ownership of the island were coming to the top through some silly little remark that had been made. She could well understand her cousin being afraid of what Philip might do about it. In her heart Judy didn't have any illusions about the way Philip felt about Rick Cartwright – Philip, the dedicated surgeon, had no patience with the playboys of the world and when they invaded his hospital, pretending to work, it didn't take much to set off the powder keg. It seemed reasonable to Judy that her cousin should ask her to go and warn Rick off about going to the island that day, since Philip's family had people out there mending the old pier. If Rick thought the place was bare and empty he might quite likely take another girl there, as he had taken Judy. And above all, Linda mustn't be upset in her present state.

The island… Judy thought about that day and of how she had been so much in love with Rick then. Rick and the island were all tied up together in her treasured memories, although the trip had been soured for her because he had in the end, treated her like any other girl until she had pulled him up.

It was raining when the taxi reached the Basin. There was the boat that Rick loved so much. She could see Rick aboard. He was busy repairing something. He always wore that striped sweater and the little wool cap, and he looked as absorbed in his task as he ought to have looked about his work in the hospital. The boat was the breath of life to him. The only other thing that could take his mind off it was the sight of a pretty girl approaching him. Judy tore down the jetty and threw herself on board as if her life depended on it. Her face was wet with the rain, her dress clung to her, and her hair turned up in funny little ducks tails all over. To Rick, who had constant negative replies, from her, she had never looked more desirable. He took her in his arms.

'Judy! How did you know I was thinking of you?' he shouted.

Her words were lost in a growl of thunder but she looked rather shocked, he thought. 'Is anything wrong?' he yelled at her.

He pulled her into the deckhouse, where it was a little more quiet. 'Now, let's mop your face. What are you doing here? You're in a shocking state, love!'

'Rick, never mind all that! Linda telephoned me – she was all worked up and crying – why did you do it?'

His face lost its fun, and set stone cold. 'What am I supposed to have done, considering I haven't been near your cousin Linda since the last time I stopped to talk to you in the garden?'

'She said you were with her today – at least, that was the impression–' Judy's voice trailed off. *Had* Linda actually said he had been with her? 'Well, anyway, she said I was to go at once to your boat and stop you going to the island because she didn't want trouble between you and Philip–' she added desperately.

'What – are – you – talking – about?' he asked, a gap between each word in sheer stupefaction. 'In the first place I am not intending to go anywhere, in dirty weather like this. In the second place, if I had been, nothing anyone (least of all your cousin Linda) could have said would have stopped me. And what makes you think I give a damn what Addison thinks? Anyway, he wouldn't biff me for going on his rotten little island, and I wouldn't bother to biff him for ordering me off, which he wouldn't. Now what is this all about, Judy?'

She smoothed her wet hair back and stared at him in stupefaction, only she wasn't looking at him but at some point he couldn't reach. 'She must be really ill,' she whispered.

'Your cousin Linda? Not she! But she's a damned good actress, I give her that! The point is, what's in it for her? Oh, stop it, Judy, can't you *see* she's setting you up as usual?'

'Why are you always saying rotten things about her?' Judy flared. 'What's she done to you?'

'The point is, what's she doing to you!' he retorted, and took Judy's hands, holding them fast. She flinched as lightning flashed across her eyes, but she was really somewhere else, going over what Linda had said. He could see that, so he tackled it from that angle. Useless to ask Judy what had been said, so he asked mildly, 'Where were you, when she telephoned you?'

'Oh, it doesn't matter! Oh, at the home of Edward Norris, one of Philip's ex-patients,' Judy said impatiently.

'Norris. H'm. I don't get this. How did she know you would be there?' he asked suddenly.

She shrugged. 'She knows I go there – I believe I told her.'

'Ah, I begin to see the light. She phones there, to get you to me so she can make sure Addison knows, because it's the one thing he will not like to hear, hating my guts as he does! Now I begin to see–'

Judy threw him off. 'You're hateful, Rick Cartwright! I don't know why I ever liked you! I must have been mad! Leave me alone – I'm going back to Linda to find out–'

'You can't go back in that storm! There's no bus anyway!' he shouted. Her voice came back, torn on the wind, something about her taxi, but the taxi had gone. He tried to tell her, running after her. 'Wait, Judy, and I'll drive you!' he called.

He couldn't see, for the driving rain, and spray dashed up and went all over the place where Judy had been running. Suddenly in a flash of lightning which lit everything up with a lurid glare he saw her, just as she slipped on the wet boards. He wasn't near enough to do anything to help her. She seemed to be tossed lightly over the side of the jetty, into the sea, where two small pleasure boats slapped their sides together...

Chapter Thirteen

This was the thing that had haunted Philip since he had first started his medical training: what if a casualty should belong to me? From the moment he was personally sent for, and heard those words: 'There's been an accident...' with the special significance underlying them, the nightmare fear of half a lifetime thrust itself forward in his mind. Judy looked like a stranger, lying on that stretcher. What clothes she had, wet and clinging, were torn and bloodstained, but his eyes riveted first on that left hand.

Thinking it over afterwards, when he and the others in his team had done all they could, he could only ask himself how it was that he hadn't been with Judy that day. Some message or other, catching him on the way out, had flung out the gearing of his free time. And then Linda had caught him, and she had been right: Judy *had* been with Rick Cartwright, on that damned boat of his.

Cartwright had been clamouring to see him but for a long time he put off the meeting. Cartwright would want to know Judy's chances. Well, he supposed he would have to see the fellow, if what Linda had hinted was true. Only somehow it all swerved another way. Linda, instead of being quietly triumphant at having been right, had gone to pieces at the news, and had to be sedated. Rick Cartwright had been quietly angry but hadn't behaved like a man in love, so much as a man in a cold malevolent fury because someone had harmed his own sister, or so it seemed to the distraught Philip and finally there had been the business of Edward Norris.

Well, he supposed he should go and see Edward first. He made the effort, but Rick Cartwright was storming along the corridor and caught him.

'Don't say "not now" to me again, sir,' Rick said between his teeth, suddenly very much the junior doctor to his senior. Such protocol from him immediately put Philip on his guard.

'Well, no, perhaps not,' he murmured. 'Perhaps this *is* the time to tell me, coldly and clearly and without frills, just what happened!'

'I was minding my own business, mending a gadget on the boat, when Judy got out of a taxi. It had started raining but she was in such a fury, she didn't even notice. She came aboard and gave me hell, all because of something *Linda* had put into her head!' Never had Rick been so clipped and to the point before, that Philip could remember. 'I can't help it, sir, if you *are* keen on Linda – she's a little toad and it's time someone stopped her mischief, because it's gone too far, as I always knew it would!'

'Now just a minute–' Philip began, not defending Linda but purely puzzled at this different aspect of everything.

'And when I tried to point this out to Judy, and make her see that damned cousin of hers in her true colours, Judy lost her temper (you know what a temper she's got, sir!) and she roared off down the jetty, shouting about going back by taxi. But her taxi hadn't waited, and anyway, she didn't reach the shore. She slipped on the planks of the jetty!'

And at that moment the telephone rang. It was Edward. 'Philip, for pity's sake tell me what's happened!' and he sounded excited, which was unusual for that cool man. 'I waited to hear from Judy and at last I telephoned the hospital and they tell me there's been an accident.'

'I'll come over, Edward,' Philip said. He mustn't let this favourite ex-patient be upset, and he'd quarrel with Rick if he stayed here. Edward said, 'I wish you would. As you know, I tape all my telephone calls. I'd just like you to hear what was said to Judy to send her rushing off like that! If I could have heard the tape before she went, I would have stopped her from going!'

In the anxious days that followed, Philip was to remember that telephone message, the harsh new voice of Linda insidiously half-saying, half suggesting, things to Judy, and knowing how they would react on her cousin. But Linda was in such a state, such a *genuine* state, that he couldn't tackle her about it, not yet.

It was a day of a three-star accident, and he was busy in theatre, when someone allowed Linda to see Judy. Linda promised to be good and quiet and was left by the bedside, but the minute she was alone, she shook Judy awake and let out the emotions that had tormented her since the accident. 'Ju, *Judy,* I didn't mean it, honestly!' she sobbed on Judy's shoulder. '*Say* it'll be all right! *Promise* it'll be all right! *Say* you'll forgive me!'

'Yes, yes, anything, only don't shake me, Lin – I hurt all over! Whatever happened to me? They won't tell me!'

'Ju, I sent you to Rick's boat, remember? Ju, I only wanted to make Philip think you were still hankering after Rick. I only wanted Edward to go off you because he's *that way* about girls who hanker after playboys like Rick – he hates them! Well, Ju, I *had* to, don't you see? You don't even *try,* you get all my fellows – and you've got everything and I've got nothing! I lost Nigel and I lost my singing voice and my speaking voice is awful, but look at what you had! Your piano playing, your bedside manner, everything! You even stopped being redhead like me, so you looked distinctive! Why didn't you stay red, Judy?'

'What ... *are* you talking about?' the bewildered Judy cried.

'It doesn't matter now,' Linda said, still sobbing, and feverishly holding Judy's right hand, tightening the grasp every so often until her nails bit into the flesh. 'It's all evened out. Philip's gone off both of us, and you won't be able to play the piano–' Linda broke off, suddenly appalled at what she had done, by the look on Judy's face. Judy's eyes went down to her left hand, it was so swathed in bandages. 'Judy, I didn't mean it! Ju, you've got to believe that! You're all I've got! Honest, I wouldn't hurt you for anything but you do see how it is, don't you? Ju, say you do!'

And then strong hands bit into her shoulders, and Philip, just out of the theatre and in no mood to be trifled with, pulled Linda to her feet and said, 'I told you no bedside scenes. Get out!' He said it very softly, and Linda, suddenly frightened, went.

He sat down by the bed, rather wearily, Judy thought.

'What can I say?' he murmured at last. 'I have protected you as far as I could, but you defeated me. You wilfully did everything to make it easy for Linda to hurt you and you wouldn't see she loves to destroy. You wouldn't see it! And I had to stand back and watch and be torn apart in the process.'

All she wanted to know was about her hand, but something in his manner claimed all her attention. He, Philip Addison, the man who was like a mountain for her to lean on, suddenly looked lost, beaten. 'I don't understand. I thought Linda had made you fall in love with her,' she said brokenly. 'You were so nice to her, always with her! I kept out of your way. There was no point...'

'Oh, my dear girl!' He buried his face in her good hand. 'I should have made you see, I suppose, but I'm not the sort of chap who can find words to say what I feel.' He looked up at her. 'I thought, as we (you and I) seemed so close, that you would *know* I wanted to protect you from people, people like Rick Cartwright ... no, you won't want to hear that from me,' he said, giving up.

'That's dead, I told you. I suppose I was in love with the person I *thought* he was. And it was easier, because you were there to lean on. Did you know that? I leaned on you until I couldn't imagine life without you to lean on and then it seemed you went over to my cousin. I think I stopped liking her then, but the habits of a lifetime can't be changed overnight. She's all I have.'

'No, she isn't,' he said, suddenly fierce. 'You've got me – if you want me!' and although it seemed to be true that he couldn't say he loved her in so many words, she didn't need to be told by the way he looked at her, or by the way he kissed her. His first kiss made her forget to ask him about her hand and the future.

After that, no day went by without Philip dropped in. He came between visits, between sessions in the theatre. He came to talk about themselves and he came to tell her of his problems. Judy made strides. She was young and healthy and her ribs healed and the bandages dwindled on the hurt hand until the time for exercise began. There were scars but Philip said hand scars heal quickly and she believed him. Other people streamed in – Thelma and her Casualty Officer, Sheila with her recuperating farmer. Everyone came to visit her but Linda. Even Judy didn't ask for Linda ... not yet. She wanted to be sure of Philip before Linda came back into her life.

Philip said one day, 'My grandmother's ring. I want you to have it instead of a formal diamond. You would like it, wouldn't you?'

She looked at her hand, wondering how

she could get it on, but Philip brought out a curious little thing like a saucer with a stunted tree growing on it. 'A Victorian ring-stand. Keep the ring on it until you're fit enough to wear it.'

She resisted the temptation to remind him that he hadn't formally proposed to her. Such a piece of information would only irritate him, since clearly he wanted nothing more than to marry her, the sooner the better. So she said, 'Philip, how beautiful, and how unusual a ring! Pearls and a ruby, and is that an emerald in the heart of the flower?'

'It is,' he said, and being Philip, he didn't even consider reminding her how much the ring was worth. She might shrink from having it, knowing Judy. He was glad Linda wasn't visiting here.

Linda went to see Felix Morford that day. 'I'm so miserable!' she said, pulling out a stool by his bedside, and forgetting he couldn't hear.

She thought this would be fairly private, as everyone had visitors and the buzz of conversation made the head ache. She was shocked when Felix said, 'Are you, love?' and some of the joy at seeing her, was obviously dashed. 'Why? Are you still feeling ill?'

Linda's jaw dropped, but Felix's neighbour stopped talking to his wife to say curtly,

'Don't worry, the poor bloke can't hear you! He's been having lip-reading training, just in case you should turn up some day!'

Linda turned on her smile again, ignored the man and told Felix all about it. 'It wasn't my fault. I just thought I was doing the right thing – that Dr Cartwright isn't right for our Judy. But they all hate me now! They won't let me see her!'

Felix had heard a different story from Philip, but in his way he was as intractable as Philip. He saw Linda as she was, with all her jealousies and insecurity, her way of hitting out at Judy if she felt Judy was eclipsing her: he understood all that, but he loved Linda all the same. Nothing would change that. He said now, 'They're all upset. Another bad thing happening to one of you girls – first you ill, then Judy. Take it in your stride, my love. It'll be all right.' And he took her hand firmly, not timidly as he had done in the past. 'Linda, I want to talk to you about something else. Are you going on with your training as a nurse?'

She had always managed to keep her feeling of disgust at the physical side of nursing well-hidden, but the question caught her off balance. She couldn't recover herself before Felix saw the truth in her face. He nodded. 'Don't say anything. I know. I've thought so all along. I can't think how you girls can bear to do half the jobs they give you to do, anyway. Especially when your first love is obviously some branch of the Arts.' He smiled and squeezed her hand. 'Listen, I get up every afternoon now, and I am going home, if...'

He broke off and looked past her. He was half aware of his neighbour's attention. He wished it could have been more private.

Linda said, wishing she hadn't come. 'How nice!' and to make conversation, she added, 'Where *is* your home?'

'That's just it!' Felix said. 'I haven't got one, *or* a family – my job took me all over the place. Now I must set about finding a home.'

She frowned. 'But will they let you leave here without a place to go to? Won't you need a nurse or something?'

'They'll let me go, if I get married,' Felix said firmly, and Linda would never know what it cost him to make the effort now, while he had her in this mood, to propose to her. 'Will you marry me? I love you very much, you must know that!'

Linda was taken aback and couldn't stop showing it. Thoughts tumbled in her mind. Nigel, the only man she had loved, was dead, and she was scared because grief still attacked her. She didn't want to feel anything so deeply. She had lost Philip, too. That had been a blow to her pride. But to marry *this* man...

Felix's neighbour couldn't resist interfering again, though his wife did her best to stop him. 'Make up your mind, girl, and put the poor bloke out of his misery. He isn't hard up – he's just been left a whacking great legacy by some relation he'd forgotten about. You won't be hard up.'

She reddened. Money had worried her, it was true.

'And he's got no family to make you toe the line,' the man in the next bed couldn't resist adding.

Linda ignored him, but what he had said did make a difference. Turning on her almost blinding smile, she said to Felix, 'I didn't know you loved me. I believe I've loved you all the time.'

Judy heard about this much later. Philip looked so worn when he came down from theatre that day, she was distressed about him.

'You need a holiday,' she said severely. 'Where do people go for a holiday when they live near the sea?'

He brightened. 'I tell you where I've always wanted to go for a holiday – there's a little island near the Bahamas, where there is sunshine all the time but it doesn't attract tourists because it's absolutely undeveloped. Nothing to do but just lie about in the sun and dream. You know, that might do you good too, love. I have the most marvellous idea. Let's spend our honeymoon there! Judy, what do you say? A quiet little wedding, no fuss, and just slide out in a plane and get away from it all?'

Her face lit, but she remembered Linda. 'Oh, my cousin–'

It was the first time she had seen Philip look really impatient. After he had said a few explosive things, he said, 'What am I going on about? I forgot to tell you! She's marrying Morford – he's inherited money and they'll let him be discharged if he gets married. And I think it's a good thing,' he finished firmly. 'She says she's in love with him!' he added in such a funny voice that they both started laughing.

'Oh, Philip, don't make me laugh – my poor ribs!'

'Don't whine, darling – your ribs are healing fine, and so is that hand. You'll even be able to play the piano again in time. You'll be fine in every way, if you trust me. You *do* trust me, don't you, my love?' he asked anxiously.

'I trust you with my life,' Judy said. 'And I'm in love with you. It's different from anything else I ever felt before,' she mused. 'Do you remember you once said I might be one of those lucky people who'd have a better time with the second falling in love?'

He nodded. 'I half hoped it would be me,' he murmured, cupping her face in his two hands before kissing her.

'Oh, it *is* you, darling Philip, it *is* you, with all my heart.'

The publishers hope that this book has given you enjoyable reading. Large Print Books are especially designed to be as easy to see and hold as possible. If you wish a complete list of our books please ask at your local library or write directly to:

Dales Large Print Books
Magna House, Long Preston,
Skipton, North Yorkshire.
BD23 4ND